John Indermaur

An Epitome of Leading Conveyancing and Equity Cases

With some short notes thereon

John Indermaur

An Epitome of Leading Conveyancing and Equity Cases
With some short notes thereon

ISBN/EAN: 9783337424978

Printed in Europe, USA, Canada, Australia, Japan

Cover: Foto ©Andreas Hilbeck / pixelio.de

More available books at **www.hansebooks.com**

AN EPITOME

OF

LEADING CONVEYANCING

AND

EQUITY CASES;

WITH SOME SHORT NOTES THEREON:

CHIEFLY INTENDED AS

A Guide to "Tudor's Leading Cases on Conveyancing," and
"White and Tudor's Leading Cases in Equity."

BY

JOHN INDERMAUR,

SOLICITOR

(1st Prizeman, Michaelmas Term, 1872),

AUTHOR OF "AN EPITOME OF LEADING COMMON LAW CASES,"
"SELF-PREPARATION FOR THE FINAL EXAMINATION,"
"PRINCIPLES OF THE COMMON LAW,"
"MANUAL OF PRACTICE,"
"SELF-PREPARATION FOR THE INTERMEDIATE EXAMINATION," &c. &c.

FIFTH EDITION.

LONDON:

STEVENS & HAYNES,

Law Publishers,

BELL YARD, TEMPLE BAR.

1884.

Ballantyne Press
BALLANTYNE, HANSON AND CO., EDINBURGH
CHANDOS STREET, LONDON

PREFACE TO FIFTH EDITION.

I HAVE in this edition chiefly confined myself to revisions rendered necessary by alterations in the law, which have been somewhat considerable. I have also in some places slightly added to and improved the notes, and given in them a few further recent cases which appeared of sufficient importance to justify me in doing so.

J. I.

22, CHANCERY LANE, W.C.
February, 1884.

INDEX TO THE CASES EPITOMIZED.

NOTE.—The edition of "TUDOR'S LEADING CASES ON CONVEYANCING," to which reference is made in this Epitome, is the 3rd, published in 1879; and the edition of "WHITE AND TUDOR'S LEADING CASES IN EQUITY," to which reference is made, is the 5th, published in 1877.

LIST OF CASES REFERRED TO IN THE NOTES.

PREFACE TO FOURTH EDITION.

In this edition I have added one principal case—viz., *Vint* v. *Padget*—for the purpose of introducing the Student to the subject of the doctrine of consolidation of mortgages. I have also added various recent cases to the notes on different subjects, and have in some particulars considerably enlarged, and I trust improved, the notes, endeavouring at the same time to keep the book down in size, that it should not cease to be what was originally intended—viz., a short Epitome of Important Cases, with some useful information thereon. I have in this edition, besides giving a list of cases epitomized, also given a list of those referred to in the notes.

J. I.

22, CHANCERY LANE, W.C.
January, 1881.

PREFACE TO THIRD EDITION.

In preparing this edition I have gone very carefully through the whole work, and have added in various particulars materially to the notes to many of the cases where, from observation with my own pupils, I have perceived that this might usefully be done. I have also been carefully through the reported cases since the publication of the last edition, and have from them chosen two additional principal ones—viz., those of *Agra Bank* (*Limited*) v. *Barry* and *Cooper* v. *Cooper*, both decided in the House of Lords, and both of very considerable importance. There are no doubt many other cases that might have been well inserted, but it is not my object to crowd too many on the Student; and I do not wish to insert any additional ones unless they are of a strikingly useful character. I trust this edition will be found to be an improvement on the last, and that the book will continue to prove useful.

In conclusion I desire to address a word of advice to the Student; and it is this: he should remember that the primary importance of his studying cases is not simply to remember the names; this is no doubt extremely useful, and especially for any one desiring to obtain " honours;" but cases are of far more importance as illustrating principles, and impressing on one's memory the law that is involved in them.   What has led me to say this is, that amongst my own pupils I have now and then found gentlemen who, with the most limited knowledge of law, have crammed up the names of cases to the neglect of the principles involved—whence sometimes confusion.

J. I.

22, CHANCERY LANE, W.C.
        April, 1877.

PREFACE TO SECOND EDITION.

———•·———

A SECOND EDITION having been called for, the Compiler
has carefully gone through the work, and enlarged the
notes in various places, and has added one additional
principal case—viz., that of *Earl Beauchamp* v. *Winn*—
on the subject of Mistake.   In the same way as has been
done in the Second Edition of the " Epitome of Leading
Common Law Cases," the reference to the original report
has been added to each case; and also for the use of
Students blank spaces are left for the purpose of making
MS. notes and additions.

22, CHANCERY LANE, W.C.
   October, 1874.

much on Conveyancing; thus, in the Final Examination at Michaelmas Term last, under the head of "Conveyancing," two questions were asked directly on Messrs. White and Tudor's Equity Cases, and it is also very convenient to consider them together.

April, 1873.

AN EPITOME

OF

LEADING CONVEYANCING

AND

EQUITY CASES.

RICHARDSON v. LANGRIDGE.

(*Lead. Cas. Conv.* 4.)

(*4 Taunt.* 128.)

Decided :—That if an agreement be made to let premises so long as both parties like, and reserving a compensation accruing *de die in diem,* and not referable to a year or any aliquot part of a year, it does not create a holding from year to year, but a tenancy at will strictly so called ; but if there is a general letting at a yearly rent, though payable half-yearly or quarterly, and though nothing is said about the duration of the term, it is an implied letting from year to year.

Notes.—Tenancies from year to year owe their origin to the inconveniences found to result from tenancies at will, which were only partially remedied by the doctrine of emblements, and the Courts at a very early period raised an implied contract for a tenancy from year to year. (Lead. Cas. Conv. 23.) The above case shews the rule for determining when a tenancy

B

is for years and when at will. The leaning of the Courts is always to construe the tenancy as from year to year. Although a tenancy may originally be at will, yet it may afterwards, by payment of rent or other circumstances, be converted into a tenancy for years (see Epitome of Lead. C. L. Cases, 5th ed. 57, 58).

The important recent case of Walsh v. Lonsdale (L. R. 21 Ch. D. 9; 46 L. T. 858) should here be noticed. This case has decided that since the Judicature Acts the rule no longer holds that a person occupying under an executory agreement for a lease is only made tenant from year to year by the payment of rent, but that he is to be treated as holding on the terms of the agreement, so that, for instance, he becomes subject to exactly the same right of distress as if a lease had been granted.

The proper notice to determine a yearly tenancy is six months, expiring at the end of the current year of the tenancy. However, under the Agricultural Holdings Act 1883 (46 & 47 Vict. c. 61), which came into operation 1 January, 1884, taking the place of the former Act of 1875, a *year's notice*, expiring at the end of the current year of the tenancy, is substituted for the usual half-year's notice (sect. 33) in those tenancies to which the Act applies—viz., tenancies wholly or in part agricultural or pastoral, or cultivated as a market-garden (sect. 54), and provided that the landlord and tenant have not, by writing under their hands, agreed that this provision shall not apply (sec. 33). A notice to quit part only of the premises included in a lease is bad, except that under provisions of the Act just mentioned (sect. 41), a notice may be given by the landlord with a view to certain uses to be made of the land in the Act specified, to be stated in the notice, which may relate to part only of the holding, but the tenant may within 28 days of the receipt of the notice, serve on the landlord a counter-notice in writing to the effect that he accepts the same as a notice to quit the entire holding at the end of the current year of the tenancy. A monthly tenancy merely requires a month's notice, and a weekly tenancy a week's notice; and in the case of lodgings a reasonable notice only is required.

LEWIS BOWLES' CASE.
(*Lead. Cas. Conv.* 37.)
(11 *Co.* 79 *b.*)

The following were the chief points resolved :—

1. That a tenant in tail, after possibility of issue extinct, shall *not* be punished for waste.

2. That if a tenant for life fells timber or pulls down the house, the lessor shall have the timber; but if the house falls down, the particular tenant has a special property in the timber to rebuild the house.

3. That a tenant for life *without impeachment of waste* has as great power to do waste and convert it at his own pleasure as has a tenant in tail.

4. That the property in severed trees vests in a tenant for life without impeachment of waste.

GARTH v. COTTON.
(1 *Lead. Cas. Eq.* 751.)
(1 *Ves.* 524, 546.)

Mr. Garth, the father of the plaintiff, was tenant of lands for ninty-nine years, if he should so long live, *without impeachment of waste, except voluntary waste;* remainder to trustees to preserve contingent remainders; remainder to his first and other sons in tail; remainder to defendant in fee. Mr. Garth (before the birth of a son) and the

defendant, according to an agreement, cut down timber
and divided the profits between them. The plaintiff was
afterwards born, and having suffered a recovery, brought
this bill against defendant to refund his share of the profits
of the timber received by him.

Decided :—That he was so entitled to recover from the
defendant.

Notes on these two Cases.—The first of the above two cases is
the leading case as to waste and the powers of persons having
estates not of inheritance; it contains several important re-
solutions, and is always referred to on the subject. The latter
case is as to that kind of waste called "equitable waste." "Waste"
is defined in Mr. Tudor's notes to *Lewis Bowles' Case* as "the
destructive or material alteration of things forming an essential
part of the inheritance;" and it is either voluntary, which is by
the tenant's own act, or permissive, as by letting the premises go
to ruin. The remedy for waste is either by action for damages
for waste already committed, or an injunction may be obtained
against future waste. An injunction cannot, however, be granted
in cases of *permissive* waste, but the party injured must be left
to his remedy for damages. Waste is also divided with reference
to the remedy into Legal and Equitable waste.

The liability of different owners for waste stands as follows :—

1. A tenant in fee simple being as nearly as can be absolute
owner of his estate, can commit any act of waste he pleases,
except indeed when there is an executory devise over, when he
cannot commit equitable waste.

2. A tenant in tail may also commit any act of waste, but if
he becomes tenant in tail after possibility of issue extinct, as
he cannot bar the entail, he is not allowed to commit equitable
waste.

3. A tenant for life is liable for all acts of voluntary waste, but
it appears not for permissive waste (Barnes *v.* Dowling, 44 L. T.
809), unless some obligation with regard to the same is specially

thrown upon him (Woodhouse *v.* Walker, L. R. 5 Q. B. D. 404);
and even when he holds his estate without impeachment of waste
he cannot commit equitable waste.

4. A tenant from year to year is also of course liable for
waste, but as to permissive waste, all he is bound to do is fair
and tenantable repairs, to keep the house wind and water tight,
not any substantial or lasting repairs.   On the other hand, the
landlord is under no liability to repair on the absence of covenant to that effect.

Voluntary waste may be committed although it does no real
injury to the inheritance, or even improves it.   This is styled
ameliorative waste, and really the liability in respect of it is more
nominal than substantial, for the Court will not usually at the
present day grant an injunction to restrain such waste (Doherty
v. Allman, L.R. 3 App. Cas. 709), but will simply leave the reversioner or remainderman to recover the damages (if any) which
he has sustained, and it is manifest that in most cases any such
damages would be but nominal.

By the Judicature Act, 1873 (36 & 37 Vict. c. 66), s. 25 (3),
it is provided that "an estate for life without impeachment of
waste shall not confer or be deemed to have conferred upon the
tenant for life any legal right to commit waste of the description
known as equitable waste, unless an intention to confer such right
shall expressly appear by the instrument creating such estate."
This is a provision arising naturally from the union of the
former Courts of Law and Equity.   Equitable waste was only
recognizable and relievable against in Equity, the principle
upon which Equity always interfered to prevent such acts being,
that an implied trust was created in favour of the person or
persons taking the ulterior interest.   Law, however, knew no
such doctrine, and suffered such acts to be committed with
impunity, and in this we find an instance of the conflict of
Law and Equity respectively.   All the former Courts being by
the Judicature Act, 1873, fused into one High Court of Justice,
it would have been an anomaly to have allowed a remedy in
the Chancery Division only.   Therefore the object of the provision is to establish uniformity in all the Divisions, and the

effect is to give a remedy for acts still known as equitable waste in every Division.

In connection with the subject of waste, the provision contained in section 35 of the Settled Land Act, 1882 (45 & 46 Vict. c. 38) should be noticed. It is as follows :—" Where a tenant for life is impeachable for waste in respect of timber, and there is on the settled land timber ripe and fit for cutting, the tenant for life, on obtaining the consent of the trustees of the settlement or an order of the Court, may cut and sell that timber or any part thereof. Three-fourths of the net proceeds of the sale shall be set aside as and be capital money arising under this Act, and the other fourth part shall go as rents and profits." See also secs. 28 (2) and 29.

TYRRINGHAM'S CASE.

(Lead. Cas. Conv. 120.)

(1 *Co.* 36 *a.*)

The following were the chief points resolved :—

1. That prescription does *not* make a thing appendant to another unless it agree in nature and quality with it, as a thing corporeal cannot be appendant to another corporeal thing, nor *vice versâ*, but a thing incorporeal may be appendant to a thing corporeal, or *è converso*; though a thing incorporeal cannot be appendant to a thing corporeal which does not agree with it in nature, so that a common of turbary cannot be appendant to land, but to a house it may. N

2. That common appendant is of common right, and need not be prescribed for; but that it only belongs to ancient arable land, and for horses and oxen to plough, and cows and sheep to manure the land.

3. Common appendant is apportionable by the commoners purchasing part of the lands to which, &c., but not common appurtenant, for there by the purchase all the common is extinguished.

4. Unity of possession of the whole land is an extinguishment of common appendant.

5. Common by vicinage is not common appendant; but inasmuch as it ought to be by prescription time out of mind, it is in this respect resembled to common appendant.

6. Common appendant remains, though a house be afterwards built on the land, or the arable land be afterwards converted into pasture; but in pleading it ought to be prescribed for as appendant to land.

Note.—The above case is the leading authority as to common and rights of common. In Mr. Tudor's notes to this case a right of common is defined as " a right which one person has of taking some part of the produce of land, while the whole property of the land itself is vested in another." There are properly four kinds of common—viz. : (1) Common of pasture ; (2) Common of piscary ; (3) Common of turbary ; and (4) Common of estovers ; and to these is sometimes added a fifth sort—viz., Common in the soil. Common of pasture, which is the most usual and important sort, may be either (1) Appendant, (2) Appurtenant, (3) Because of vicinage, or (4) In gross. A person acquires a Right of Common either by grant or by prescription. As to a grant, that speaks for itself; and with regard to prescription, that presupposes a grant. There is a considerable difference between prescription and custom. " In the Common Law," says Lord Coke, "*prescription* which is personal is for the most part applied to persons, being made in the name of a certain person and of his ancestors, or of those whose estate he has; or in bodies politic or corporate and their predecessors ; but a *custom* which is *local* is alleged in no person, but laid within some manor or other place." A prescription to take a profit in another's lands—*e.g.*, to work quarries —is good; but a custom to that effect, except in the case of copyholders or to search for and work mines under a local custom, is clearly bad, for it must have been illegal to commence with, and with regard to copyholders any custom must be reasonable. (Lead. Cases, Conv. 137.)

Formerly the right to common by prescription could be defeated by shewing that enjoyment commenced since the beginning of the reign of Richard I. (for the reason for which see Best on Evidence, 480, quoted in Goodeve's Modern Law of Real Property, 354); but now under the Prescription Act the time for which a right of common must be enjoyed, to constitute a good title to it, is, that it must be held for thirty years, after which it is only defeasible by reason of disability, and after sixty years it is indefeasible unless the holding be by consent given by deed or writing (2 & 3 Will. 4, c. 71). This statute has not altered the nature of the right, or the principles upon which it is to be determined whether the right has been infringed, but has merely substituted a statutory title for the previous fictitious one (per *Lord Selborne* in *City of London Brewery Co.* v. *Tennant*, L. R. 9 Ch. App. 219 ; per *James L. J.* in *Kelk* v. *Parsons*, L. R. 6 Ch. App. 809 ; Goodeve's Modern Law of Real Property, 356).

SURY v. PIGOT.

(*Lead. Cas. Conv.* 154.)

(*Poph.* 166.)

The following were the chief points determined :—

1. That a watercourse having its origin *ex jure naturæ*, and not from grant or prescription, is not extinguished by unity of possession; but

2. A right of way having its origin either by grant or prescription will be extinguished by unity of possession unless it be a way of necessity, as a way to market or church.

3. Where a person has a house and ancient windows in it, and another person erects a new house and stops up the light, an action will lie.

Notes.—This case is the leading authority upon the law of easements. An easement is defined by Mr. Tudor in his notes to the case as " a right which the owner of one tenement, which is called the dominant tenement, has over another, which is called the servient tenement, to compel the owner thereof to permit to be done, or to refrain from doing, something on such tenement for the advantage of the former." Easements may arise by express or implied grant, or by prescription, or by Act of Parliament.

An easement may be either affirmative, or a right of way; or negative, or a right to light.

The time for which enjoyment of an easement must be had to constitute a good title was formerly the same as with regard to a right of common (*ante*, p. 8), but it is now fixed by the same statute as applies to rights of common—viz., 2 & 3 Will. 4, c. 71. By that statute twenty years' uninterrupted enjoyment is to confer a title, except in the case of disability, and the right is to be absolute after forty years unless the holding is by consent given by deed or writing.   In the one case of light the right is to be absolute after twenty years.   See as to the effect of this statute, *ante*, p. 9.

The chief ways in which an easement may be extinguished are as follows: By unity of possession; by the authority of Act of Parliament; by release under seal; and by the abandonment of the enjoyment of the easement by non-user.   The case itself, although a general authority on the subject of easement, yet goes, it will be noticed, particularly to the point of extinguishment of easements, shewing that easements will be extinguished by unity of possession, except where the easement is one actually of necessity, or it is some right arising *ex jure naturæ*.   With regard to what will constitute an abandonment of a right of this kind, it is not necessary to show any definite period of non-user, but what period is sufficient must depend on all the surrounding circumstances of the case (Goodeve's Modern Law of Real Property, 352).

A person can only gain a right to a view or prospect by grant, covenant, or contract, and not by prescription (see further as to easements, Goodeve's Modern Law of Real Property, 350–359).

FOX v. BISHOP OF CHESTER.

(*Lead. Cas. Conv.* 238.)

(6 *Bing.* 1.)

Here, whilst the incumbent of the living was *in extremis*, but before he died, the next presentation was sold, but without the privity of, and without any intention to present, the particular clerk to the church when vacant.

Decided :—That this sale was not void on the ground of simony.

Notes.—But had the sale been when the living was actually vacant, it would have been simoniacal and bad. Simony is an offence consisting in the corrupt and unlawful presentation to a living, and this case may be quoted generally on the point, and also particularly as shewing how far one may go without being guilty of simony. But although a next presentation may be sold whilst the incumbent is living, yet it is simoniacal to pur-chase it with the intention of presenting any particular person. A person also cannot purchase a next presentation and present himself. An advowson is real property, but the next presentation is personal property.

It may be useful to here notice the subject of Resignation Bonds. These are bonds executed by a minister who is appointed to a living when he agrees to resign it in a certain person's favour, and they are frequently had recourse to when the patron has some relative he may wish to present the living to, but who is not yet ordained, or some other circumstances render it impossible for him to take to the living at once. A general resignation bond is bad, but by 9 Geo. 4, c. 94, such a bond is to be good if in favour of any one person named, *or* one of two persons, each being by blood or marriage an uncle, son, grandson, brother, nephew, or grand-nephew of the patron or one of the patrons. One part of the instrument by which the engagement is made must be deposited within two calendar months in the office of the registrar of the diocese, and the resignation when made must refer to the engagement, and state for whose benefit it is made.

TYRRELL'S CASE.

(*Lead. Cas. Conv.* 335.)

(*Dyer*, 155 *a.*)

Decided :—That there cannot be a use upon a use.

Notes.—The Statute of Uses (27 Hen. 8, c. 10) provided, that where any persons should stand seised of any hereditaments to the use, confidence, or trust of any other persons, &c., the persons, &c., who had any such use, confidence, or trust should be deemed in lawful seisin and possession of the same hereditaments for such estates as they had in the use, trust, or confidence. The above case decided that the statute executing the first use declared, subsequent uses were void; and it was in consequence of this that the Court of Chancery stepped in, and thus arose the modern doctrine of uses and trusts.

Whilst considering this case the student should bear in mind why it was that lands were previously to the passing of the Statute of Uses so commonly conveyed to uses. There were three prominent advantages gained by so conveying lands—viz. : (1) The use, unlike the estate, was not liable to be forfeited for treason. (2) The use might be given to a charity. (3) Though the legal estate could not be disposed of by will, the land could be conveyed to such uses as should be appointed by will, and a will then made of the use. The object of the Statute of Uses was of course to put an end to the practice which had previously existed by conveying lands to uses. Practically, however, by the decision in the above case, and the consequent holding of the Court of Chancery, the object of the Statute of Uses was frustrated. The immediate real effect of the statute may be illustrated thus :—If it were desired that A. should be constituted trustee of land for B., it would before the Statute have been limited to A. to the use of B. Now, however, it would be limited unto and to the use of A. to the use of B. In this case, though A. is no doubt in by the common law, yet the giving to him also of a use makes the use to B. a subsequent or second use, and gives to B. the equitable or beneficial estate.

The Statute of Uses speaks only of one man being seised to the use of another; if therefore land is limited "unto and to the use of A. and his heirs," though A. take the legal estate, it is not by force of the Statute of Uses, but by force of the Common Law. The declaration of a use here, however, prevents the possibility of any resulting use to the grantor. If it were a voluntary conveyance "unto A. and his heirs" simply, the use, and consequently the legal estate, would result to the grantor; adding the words "and to the use of" prevents this.

It must be recollected that there are three modes of conveyance which operate only over the use and do not pass the legal estate; that is to say, that although the person named gets the legal estate, it is not by any conveyance of the property, but by the force of the Statute—viz. : (1) A bargain and sale; (2) A covenant to stand seised; and (3) An appointment under a power. Thus, if a person having a power of appointment over land appoints to "A. to the use of B," here A. has the legal estate and B. the equitable.

ALEXANDER v. ALEXANDER.

(*Lead. Cas. Conv.* 395.)
(2 *Ves.* 610.)

Here, under a power to appoint amongst children the appointer had appointed part to children and part to grandchildren.

Decided :—That the appointment to grandchildren was bad ; but that a power may be good and bad in part, and the excess only void, where the execution is complete and the bounds between it and the excess clear.

TOLLET v. TOLLET.

(1 *Lead. Cas. Eq.* 254.)
(2 *P. Wms.* 489.)

Here a husband had a power to make a jointure to his wife by deed, and he did it by will, and she had no other provision.

Decided :—That Equity will make this defective execution good ; but that it would not assist in the case of non-execution of a power.

ALEYN v. BELCHIER.

(1 *Lead. Cas. Eq.* 415.)
(1 *Eden,* 132.)

Here a power of jointuring was executed in favour of a wife, but with an agreement that the wife should only receive a part as an annuity for her own benefit, and that the residue should be applied to the payment of the husband's debts.

Decided :—That this was a fraud upon the power, and the execution was set aside, except so far as related to the annuity, the bill containing a submission to pay it, and only seeking relief against the other objects of the appointment.

TOPHAM v. DUKE OF PORTLAND.

(1 *De G. J. & S.* 517.)

Here the donee of a power, appointing portions in pursuance thereof, appointed a double share to one of the objects of the power without any previous communication with him, but the instructions with reference to such double share were that half should be held upon a certain trust; and soon after the appointment the appointee executed a deed settling the moiety accordingly.

Decided :—That the purpose of the appointment as to the moiety, though uncommunicated, vitiated it as to that portion, but as to that portion only. The rights of persons entitled in default of appointment under a power can be defeated only by its *bonâ fide* exercise.

Notes on these four Cases.—These cases are here placed together for convenience as all bearing on the same general subject, the first as to the result of an excessive execution of a power, the second as shewing that Equity will assist in the case of defective execution of a power, and the remaining two as being both leading authorities as to what acts will be considered frauds upon powers.

With regard to the first case given—viz., that of *Alexander* v.

C

Alexander, it has been decided upon the principle of *cy près* that where a power of appointing land, or money to be laid out in land, is given in favour of children, and the power is extended by will in favour of a child for life with remainder to the children of such child in tail, here the Court will give an estate tail to the child to whom only a life estate is given by the will. This, however, has no application to personalty not directed to be laid out in the purchase of land, and it only applies to wills (Sugden on Powers, 8th ed. 498–503.)

With regard to the defective execution of a power relief will be given in Equity in favour of any of the following:— (1) A charity; (2) A purchaser; (3) A creditor; (4) An *intended* husband; (5) A wife; (6) A legitimate child; where in each case the defect is not of the very essence of the power. Notwithstanding the decision in *Tollet* v. *Tollet*, that relief will not be given in the case of non-execution of a power, there are two cases in which such relief will be given—viz.: (1) Where the execution has been prevented by fraud; and (2) Where the power is coupled with a trust; and an instance of the latter exception appears in the case of *Harding* v. *Glynn* (*post*, p. 20), though the principal decision in that case was on another point.

Powers with regard to land may be described as methods of causing a use with its accompanying estate to spring up at the will of any given person (Wms. Real Property, 14th ed. 308). They have been divided as of three kinds—viz., Appendant, In gross, and Collateral. A power appendant is where the person to whom the power is given has an interest in the estate to which it is annexed; a power in gross is where a person having an interest in the land has power to create an estate therein, but only to take effect after the determination of his own interest. Both powers appendant and in gross may be defeasanced or released. Powers collateral are those given to persons taking no interest in the land, and are in the nature of trusts, so that they cannot be extinguished or destroyed, and Equity will give assistance in the case of non-execution of such powers (see Tudor's Lead. Cas. Conv.).

Powers may also be divided into General and Special Powers,

the former being where there is a general power to appoint in favour of any person, and the latter where the appointment is limited to a particular class; and with regard to this division there is the following important difference as regards the rule against perpetuities—viz., general powers having no tendency to perpetuity, the time of vesting is reckoned, not from the creation but from the execution of the power; but special powers having such a tendency, the time of vesting runs from the instrument creating the power (1 Sugd. Powers, 8th ed. 394–397).

Upon the subject of Powers it may be well to notice the law as to Illusory appointments as appertaining closely to frauds upon powers. An Illusory appointment is where a person having a power to appoint amongst a certain class, appoints to all the members of such class, but only giving nominal shares to one or more members. An Illusory appointment was originally valid at Law, but not in Equity, on the ground that such an appointment was not an execution of the power *bonâ fide* for the end intended by the donor; but by the 1 Wm. 4, c. 46, it was provided that an Illusory appointment should be valid and effectual in Equity as well as at Law. And now a recent statute (37 & 38 Vict. c. 37) has carried the matter still further, providing that no appointment shall be invalid merely on the ground that any object of the power has been altogether excluded, unless indeed the instrument creating the power expressly declares the amount or the share of any object of the power, or that any object of the power is not to be excluded.

The Conveyancing Act, 1881 (44 & 45 Vict. c. 41, sect. 52), now provides that a person to whom any power is given, whether coupled with an interest or not, may by deed release or contract not to exercise it. The Conveyancing Act, 1882 (45 & 46 Vict. c. 39, sect. 6), also provides that any such person may disclaim a power, and thereafter shall become incapable of exercising it or joining in its exercise, and that on such disclaimer the power may be exercised by the other or others, or the survivors or survivor of the others, of the persons to whom the power is given, unless the contrary is expressed in the instrument creating the power. Both of these enactments are retrospective.

HARDING v. GLYNN.

(2 *Lead. Cas. Eq.* 946.)

(1 *Atk.* 469.)

A testator by his will gave personal property to his wife, but *did desire her,* at or before her death, to give the same unto and among such of his own relations as she should think most deserving and approve of.

Decided:—That the wife was only intended to take beneficially during her life, and that so much of the property not disposed of in accordance with the power ought to be divided equally amongst such of the relations of the testator as were his next of kin at the time of his wife's death.

Notes.—In the above case words which merely expressed the wish or desire of the testator were held to constitute a trust, and frequently it is very difficult to determine when and when not a trust will be created by words of that nature. The general rule is, that where property is given absolutely, accompanied with words of recommendation, entreaty, or wish that the donee will dispose of that property in favour of another, such words shall be held to create a trust; but (1) the words must be so used that upon the whole they ought to be construed as imperative; (2) the subject of the recommendation or wish must be certain; and (3) the objects of the recommendation or wish must be certain. Such Trusts are called Precatory Trusts. Words of recommendation, &c., will *not* be construed as imperative if an intention appear in any part of the will to give the devisee a right or power to spend the property.

Precatory trusts come properly under the definition of Express trusts, these being defined as trusts clearly expressed by the author or creator, or capable of being fairly collected from a written document. They cannot of course be said to be clearly expressed, but yet on a correct interpretation of the whole instrument they may fairly be collected from it.

CADELL v. PALMER.

(*Lead. Cas. Conv.* 424.)

(1 *Clark & Finelly*, 372.)

Decided:—That a limitation by way of executory devise, which is not to take effect until after the determination of a life or lives in being, and a term of twenty-one years as a term in gross, and without reference to the infancy of any person, is a valid limitation ; a period for gestation to be allowed in those cases in which it actually exists ; but not otherwise.

GRIFFITHS v. VERE.

(*Lead. Cas. Conv.* 497.)

(9 *Ves.* 127.)

Decided :—That a trust by will for accumulation during a life, contrary to the Thellusson Act (39 & 40 Geo. 3, c. 98), is good for twenty-one years by that statute.

Notes on these two Cases.—In *Cadell* v. *Palmer* the limits of the rule against perpetuities were finally ascertained and marked out, and no limitation will be held good which under any possible event may exceed its limit except that no period is too remote for the limitation of an executory estate or interest engrafted on an estate tail previously limited, the reason being that it is always liable to be barred by the tenant in tail, and therefore the remoteness of the event on which it depends does not suspend the absolute ownership of the property so as to effect a perpetuity (Goodeve's Modern Law of R. P. 224). By the Conveyancing Act, 1882 (45 & 46 Vict. c. 39, sect. 10), it is provided that where in any instrument coming into operation after 31 December, 1882, an executory limitation is created in default of failure of the issue of a person to whom an estate is given, that executory limitation shall become void and incapable of taking effect if and as soon as there is living any issue who has attained the age of twenty-one years. Thus if an estate is devised " to A., but if he shall die without issue, to B.," A., under 1 Vict. c. 26 (sect. 29), takes a fee simple, subject to an executory devise over to B., but directly A. has a child who attains the age of twenty-one years, the executory limitation over is at an end, and A.'s estate is absolute and indefeasible.

The accumulation of the income of property, and the suspension of all enjoyment of it, might formerly be directed for the same period as the suspension of its alienation or vesting; but in consequence of the extraordinary will of Mr. Thellusson, which provided for the accumulation of the income of his property for a long period, but yet strictly within the time allowed for the creation of executory interests, the statute 39 & 40 Geo. 3, c. 98, commonly known as " The Thellusson Act," was passed. This statute forbids the accumulation of income for any longer than one of the following periods—viz. : (1) The life or lives of the grantor or grantors, settlor or settlors; or (2) The term of twenty-one years from the death of any such grantor, settlor, devisor, or testator; or (3) During the minority or respective minorities of any person or persons who shall be living or in *ventre sa mère* at the time of the death of such grantor, devisor, or testator; or (4) During the minority or respective minorities only of any person or persons who under the deed, surrender, will, or other assurance directing such accumulations, would for the time being, if of full age, be entitled to the rents, issues, and profits, or the interest, dividends, or annual produce so directed to be accumulated. *Griffiths* v. *Vere* is the leading case upon the construction of this statute, and shews that although the trust for accumulation may exceed the periods allowed by this statute, yet it shall be good for twenty-one years. But it is important to remember that if a direction to accumulate income exceeds the limit allowed for the creation of executory interests, it is altogether void, and *not* good even for the twenty-one years. The reason is, that this would have been so before the 39 & 40 Geo. 3, c. 98, and that statute is *not* an enabling, but a restraining Act only.

Section 2 of 39 & 40 Geo. 3, c. 98, provides that nothing therein contained shall extend to (1) any provision for payment of debts, or (2) any provision for raising portions for any child or children of any grantor, settlor, or devisor, or any child or children of any person taking any interest under any such conveyance, settlement, or devise; or (3) any direction touching the produce of timber or wood upon any lands or tenements.

In every case in which an accumulation is directed contrary to the above-mentioned Act the direction is null and void, and the rents and profits, so long as they are directed to be accumulated contrary to the provisions of the Act, go to such person or persons as would have been entitled thereto if such accumulation had not been directed; which does *not* mean that it will go to the person entitled after the accumulation unless otherwise entitled (Goodeve's Modern Law of R. P. 100). This is well shewn by the recent case of *Weatherall* v. *Thornburgh* (L. R. 8 Ch. D. 261), where a man devised an estate to trustees in trust for his wife for life or until second marriage, and in case of second marriage directed the income to be accumulated during the remainder of her life, and then gave the remainder with accumulations after her death to a stranger. This clearly exceeded the period allowed by the Act, and the accumulative direction was therefore void in respect of any excess over twenty-one years from the testator's death. The widow married again, and it was held that there was an intestacy as to the accumulations during the period between twenty-one years from the testator's death and the death of his widow, and that his heir took for the rest of the life of the testator's wife.

By 40 & 41 Vict. c. 33, certain limitations which might have failed as contingent remainders are to take effect as executory interests.

That statute enacts as follows: " Every contingent remainder created by any instrument executed after the passing of this Act, or by any will or codicil revived or republished by any will or codicil executed after that date, in tenements or hereditaments of any tenure, *which would have been valid as a springing or shifting use or executory devise or other limitation*, had it not had a sufficient estate to support it as a contingent remainder, shall in the event of the particular estate determining before the contingent remainder vests, be capable of taking effect in all respects as if the contingent remainder had originally been created as a springing or shifting use or executory devise or other executory limitation." The words italicised in this enactment should be carefully noticed, and the effect of the enactment may be thus instanced :—Devise " to A. for life and then to his first son who shall attain twenty-one years." This is a limitation good either as a contingent remainder or an executory interest. If when A. dies he has a son aged twenty-one, it will take effect as a remainder ; but if, though he has a son, he has not yet attained twenty-one, though failing as a contingent remainder, the statute preserves it as an executory interest. But suppose the limitation were " to A. for life, and then to his first son who shall attain twenty-five years": this is quite good as a contingent remainder, and the son will take if he is twenty-five at A.'s decease ; but suppose he is not, then it fails as a contingent remainder, and the above statute cannot preserve it, for it is a void limitation as an executory interest.

CORBYN v. FRENCH.

(*Lead. Cas. Conv.* 519.)

(4 *Tes.* 418.)

John Brown by his will bequeathed £500 to the trustees of a chapel, to be applied by them towards the discharge of a mortgage on the said chapel.

Decided :—That this legacy was void under 9 Geo. 2, c. 36.

Notes.—Statutes of Mortmain have been passed from very early times, their policy being to protect the interests of the feudal lords, the earliest enactments being Magna Charta, which prohibited alienation in Mortmain, and the statute *De Religiosis* (7 Ed. 1, st. 2), still further prohibiting evasions of the prior enactment. The ingenuity of ecclesiastics still triumphed, however, by the idea of Uses, a device only defeated by 15 Rich. 2, c. 5, which statute also applied the doctrine to corporations generally.

But the Crown has almost from time immemorial had the power, as part of its prerogative, to grant licences to hold land in Mortmain, and charters of incorporation usually contain such powers. Similar powers may also be given by statute—*e.g.*, is the case with regard to joint stock companies (25 & 26 Vict. c. 89).

The statute now known as the Mortmain Act is the one referred to in the above decision—viz., statute 9 Geo. 2, c. 36, which provides that no land or money or stock to be laid out in purchasing land shall be settled for charitable uses unless (1) by deed indented, sealed, and delivered in the presence of two or more witnesses; (2) executed twelve calendar months before death of grantor; (3) enrolled in Chancery within six calendar months after execution; and (4) made to take effect in possession immediately from the making, without any reservation or limitation for the benefit of grantor or any person claiming under him, and as to such stock unless it shall be transferred six calendar months before the death of the grantor. But in the case of a purchase for valuable consideration actually paid *at or before the making* of the conveyance or transfer, the provisions for execution twelve calendar months before grantor's death, and transfer of stock six calendar months before death are not, to apply. Gifts to either of the two universities, or to the colleges of Eton, Winchester, or Westminster, for the better support of the scholars upon the foundations of such colleges, are excepted from the operation of the statute.

24 Vict. c. 9, does away with the necessity of indenting the deed, and allows of the reservation of a nominal rent and some other reservations, and provides that the assurance shall not be void by reason, in the case of a sale for full and valuable consideration, of such consideration consisting wholly or in part of a rent-charge or other annual payment. But in all reservations allowed by the Act the vendor must reserve the same benefit for his representatives as for himself.

Although this Act allowed the valuable consideration to consist of a rent-charge, yet there was nothing in it to preserve a conveyance reserving such rent from becoming void by the decease of the vendor within twelve calendar months from the date of the deed. 27 Vict. c. 13, therefore provides that any full and valuable consideration, consisting in whole or in part of a rent or other annual payment, shall be as valid as if actually paid at or before the making of the conveyance.

33 & 34 Vict. c. 34, provides that all corporations and trustees holding moneys in trust for any public or charitable purpose may invest in real securities without being deemed to have infringed the Mortmain Act.

34 Vict. c. 13 (The Public Parks Act, 1871), exempts from the operation of the Mortmain Act gifts and bequests of land, or money to purchase lands, for the purposes of (1) Parks; (2) Schoolhouses or elementary schools; and (3) Public museums; but provides that the instrument, if voluntary, must be executed twelve calendar months before the death of the testator or

grantor, and be enrolled with the Charity Commissioners within
six months after coming into operation ; and gifts by will are
limited to twenty acres for one park, two acres for one museum,
and one acre for one schoolhouse.

35 & 36 Vict. c. 24, provides for the incorporation of trustees
of charities by application to the Charity Commissioners, and for
their then becoming a corporate body with perpetual succession,
and with power to acquire and hold property ; but it expressly
provides (s. 1) that nothing therein contained shall be taken or
construed to extend, modify, or control any of the provisions of
9 Geo. 2, c. 36, or to make valid any gift, grant or purchase
which would be invalid under that Act.

The above are the most important statutes on the subject of
Mortmain ; but further exceptions to the Mortmain Act exist in
favour of sites for schools, literary and scientific institutions, and
some other objects.

The student should give particular attention to the provisions
of the Public Parks Act, 1871.

The subject of "superstitious uses" is sometimes confounded
with that of "Mortmain," but the two are distinct, though they
may be equally void ; but whilst a gift of land to a charity, if it
is void, is so by reason of infringing the 9 Geo. 2, c. 36, as in
Corbyn v. *French*, a gift for a superstitious use is void by reason
of the old law irrespective of that Act. Thus a gift for the
erection of a monument to a testator, or for the repair of a
tomb or vault to hold his remains, or for the interment of
his family, is not charitable, and therefore a gift of land for any
such purpose is not void under 9 Geo. 2, c. 36, but as being for
a superstitious use (Goodeve's Modern Law of R. P. 95, 96).

THE RULE IN SHELLEY'S CASE.

(*Lead. Cas, Conv.* 589.)

(1 *Co.* 93 *b.*)

Decided :—That where the ancestor takes an estate of freehold, and in the same gift or conveyance an estate is limited, either mediately or immediately, to his heirs or the heirs of his body, the word " heirs" is a word of limitation, and not of purchase ; so that the ancestor takes the whole estate comprised in the term : that is to say, in the first case, an estate in fee simple ; in the second, an estate in fee tail.

Notes.—The above "Rule in *Shelley's Case*"applies to equitable as well as legal estates ; but where one limitation is legal and the other equitable it does *not* apply. Thus a grant unto and to the use of A. for life with remainder to the heirs or heirs of the body of A. gives A. a fee simple or fee tail as the case may be, and if an intermediate estate to a third party were given after the life estate to A. and before the limitation to his heirs or heirs of the body, the result would be the same, subject to the intervening estate ; but if the grant is unto and to the use of A. for life with remainder to the use of B. and his heirs in trust for the heirs or heirs of the body of A., here A. would take but a life estate, and his heirs or heirs of the body would take as purchasers.

The meaning of the rule is simple and apparent enough—viz., that where there is a gift to a person and his heirs or the heirs of his body, it is not to be taken as conferring any estate on the heir, but simply shewing or marking out the estate that the ancestor takes. And this is so although there may be an intervening estate between the gift of freehold to the ancestor and the subsequent limitation to the heirs. The rule is of very ancient origin.

The rule in *Shelley's Case* has of course no application to personal property, but with regard to personal property a rule has sprung up similar to it : thus, if personalty is settled in trust for A. for life, and after his decease in trust for his executors, administrators, and assigns, A. will simply be entitled absolutely. There cannot in fact be estates in personal property, and the only exception is a bequest of a term of years to one for life and then to another, which is allowed. The only course is to vest the property in trustees on trust. If leaseholds were settled simply on trusts to correspond with the uses of freeholds in a strict settlement, the result would be that they would vest absolutely in the first tenant in tail immediately upon his birth. This is usually avoided in practice by means of a trust for sale and for reinvestment in the purchase of freeholds to be settled, the same uses as the settled freeholds, with power to postpone the sale, and a direction that the rents and enjoyment until sale shall belong to the persons who would be entitled to the rents of the substituted freeholds (Goodeve's Modern Law of R. P. 38, 79, 80; see also notes to *Leventhorpe* v. *Ashbie, post*, p. 36).

WILD'S CASE.

(*Lead. Cas. Conv.* 669.)
(6 *Co.* 16 *b.*)

Decided :—That where there is a devise to a person and his children or issue and he has no issue at the time of the devise, there such person will take an estate tail, but if he has issue at the time he and his children take joint estates.

Notes.—This decision is known as the " Rule in *Wild's Case*," and the reason of it is, that as the devisor evidently intended that the devisee's children should take, and they cannot take as immediate devisees, for they are not in existence, nor by way of remainder, because that was not intended; the words shall be taken as words of limitation.

However, the rule in *Wild's Case* is of a flexible character, and will yield to a contrary intention appearing upon the face of the will. As an instance of this may be taken the somewhat recent case of *Grieve* v. *Grieve*, L. R. 4 Eq. 180. There a testator devised a house to his nieces and to their children, and if they had not any, then to their brother William and his children; the furniture to go with the house. Neither of the nieces had a child at the date of the will, and it was held that the rule in *Wild's Case* being flexible and yielding to the intention of the testator, the nieces took the house and furniture for their lives, with immediate remainders to the children of each coming into *esse* during the lives of the nieces. The following extract from the judgment shews the principle on which this decision was based :—" By giving an estate tail the testator's intention would be defeated. The rule in *Wild's Case* may be departed from, and in this case the direction that the furniture shall go with the house appears to me to be sufficient reason for not giving estates tail. The devise of the house and the gift of the furniture must be taken together, and by holding that the children take as purchasers, the intention of the testatrix will be carried out as far as is consistent with the rules of law."

GARDNER v. SHELDON.

(*Lead. Cas. Conr.* 625.)

(*Vaughan*, 259.

Decided :—That a devise to B. after the death of A. gives A. an estate for life by implication *if B. be heir-at-law* of testator ; but no estate if he be not heir-at-law.

An heir-at-law cannot be disinherited except by necessary implication.

Notes.—The reason of the above decision is, that if B. is not the heir-at-law, it might possibly be considered that the testator intended that during A.'s life the property should descend to his heir-at-law ; but if the subsequent devise be to the heir-at-law, it could not be so considered. However, even in this case no estate by implication will arise if there be a residuary devise, for then it would be considered that it was meant that the residuary devisee was intended to take.

An estate by implication of law takes place only in limitations of uses, either by assurances operating merely by the statute, or by the medium of a conveyance to serve the uses, and in dispositions by will ; for as is indeed laid down by the above case, "the law (that is the Common Law) does not in *conveyances* of estates, admit of estates to pass by implication regularly, as being a way of passing estates not agreeable to the plainness required by law in transferring estates from one to another." (Leading Cases Conv. 640.)

On the same principle cross-remainders cannot be implied in a deed, but in a will they may be raised by implication, on the ground that the testator being *inops concilii*, by construction his words ought to be made to answer his intent appearing in other parts of his will as nearly as may be.

D

VINER v. FRANCIS.

(*Lead. Cas. Conv.* 798.)

(2 *Cox*, 190.)

Here a testator bequeathed unto the children of his late sister the sum of £2,000, to be equally divided among them, and the question was, what children should take?

Decided :—That those children should take who were living at the death of the testator.

Notes.—It may be useful here to state shortly the rules for construction of testamentary gifts to children :—

(1.) That an immediate gift to children, whether of a living or a deceased person, comprehends all those living at testator's death, and those only.

(2.) That where a particular interest is carved out, with a gift over to the children of any person, such gift will embrace not only those living at testator's death, but all who come into existence before the period of distribution.

(3.) That where the period of distribution is postponed until the attainment of a given age by the children, the gift will apply to all who come into existence before the first child attains that age, but only to those. (See *Gimblett* v. *Purton*, L. R. 12 Eq. 427; *In re Gardiner's Estate*, L. R. 20 Eq. 647.)

(4.) That where there is an immediate gift to children by will, and at the period when distribution takes place there are no children in existence, all the children born at any future period will take.

(5.) The words "to be born" will have the effect of extending the gift to all the children who shall ever come into existence. (2 Jarman on Wills, 4th ed. 154–167.)

With regard to the 3rd rule given above, it must be

remembered that it is a rule of convenience, and that as there is much injustice in excluding, for the mere sake of the convenience of others, those children born after the eldest one of them attains the given age, the Court is not inclined to extend the operation of the rule.   (Lead. Cas. Conv. 805.)

LEVENTHORPE v. ASHBIE.

(*Lead. Cas. Conv.* 861.)
(*Rolle's Abr.* 831, *pl.* 1.)

A. devised a term of years to B. and the heirs male of his body begotten.

Decided :—That B. was absolutely entitled to the term, and that on his death it went to his executors.

Notes.—It is now well established, in accordance with the above case, that a bequest to a person of chattels, whether real or personal, in such terms as would in the case of a devise of real estate have conferred upon him an estate tail, will as a general rule give him an absolute interest, which on his death will go, not to his heir in tail, but to his personal representative. There can, indeed, in personal property be no estate, for such property is essentially the subject of absolute ownership, and besides the fact of a grant to one and the heirs of his body conferring an absolute interest, so even if any chattel be assigned to one for his life, that person will at once become entitled at law to the whole, and this would be so even were the chattel a term of years of any length.

To this rule there is an exception in the case of a bequest of a term of years to one for life, for on the death of the legatee for life the term is held to shift away and to vest in the person next entitled by way of executory bequest; and although the above-mentioned strict doctrine of the indivisibility of chattels was retained in the Courts of Law, yet in modern times it was not observed in Equity, for there the object has always been to carry out the intention of the parties; and if a chattel is given to A. for life, and afterwards to B., B. has a vested interest in remainder which he may dispose of at pleasure; and if moveable goods were thus given, the Court would compel the life owner to furnish and sign an inventory of the goods, and undertake to take proper care of them. With regard to this difference between Law and Equity, the student will remember that the rules of Equity now prevail. (Judicature Act, 1873, sect. 25, sub-sect. 11.) However, if a gift is made of articles *quæ ipso usu consumuntur*, as wines, &c., this will always vest in the first donee the absolute interest (see also hereon notes to *Shelley's Case, ante,* p. 29.)

With regard to a gift of personalty to one for life and then to another, such a gift of specific personalty must be distinguished from a gift as a whole or as a residue. (As to the rule in that case, see *Howe* v. *Earl of Dartmouth, post,* p. 106.)

ELLIOTT v. DAVENPORT.

(*Lead. Cas. Conv.* 902.)

(1 *P. Wms.* 83.)

Testatrix by her will bequeathed unto Sir William Elliott, his executors, administrators, and assigns, the sum of £100 which he owed her, provided that he should thereout pay several sums to his children; and she directed her executors to deliver up the security and not to claim any part of the debt, but to give such release as the said Sir William Elliott should think fit. Sir W. Elliott died in the lifetime of testatrix.

Decided :—That this was a lapsed legacy; and it was admitted on both sides and agreed to by the Court, that the mere addition of the words "executors, administrators, and assigns," will not prevent a lapse, for they are but surplusage.

Notes.—The same doctrine applies to a limitation to a man "and his heirs." A mere declaration that a gift shall not lapse will have no effect if there be no substitution for the person dying in testator's lifetime; but *if, together with such a declaration*, the gift is to a person and his executors, &c., this will prevent a lapse. The intention of substitution also will be implied, and a lapse thus prevented, where there is a gift to a person "*or*" his personal representatives.

It must be borne in mind that by 1 Vict. c. 26, ss. 32 & 33, no lapse is to occur (1) in the case of the devise of an estate tail where any issue are living at testator's death who would be inheritable under such entail, and (2) in the case of a devise or bequest to a child or other issue of the testator who dies leaving issue living at testator's death.

With regard to this second case, the effect of the provision is not necessarily to make the child of the child take, but to render the subject of the devise or bequest the absolute property of the deceased devisee or legatee. The effect of the provision is well shewn by two recent cases—viz., *Eager* v. *Furnivall* (L. R. 17 Ch. D. 115); and *In re Hensler*, deceased, *Jones* v. *Hensler* (L. R. 19 Ch. D. 612; 51 L. J. Ch. 303). In this latter case a testator devised property to his son, who died during his lifetime, leaving issue, and having devised all his real estate to his father, the testator. It was held that the son took the property under the 33rd section of the Wills Act, as he must by force of that provision be deemed to have survived his father, and on this principle, that though his father actually survived him, yet he must be deemed to have died before him, so that the devise in the son's will failed, and the estate went to the son's heir, who of course was his child; but this child took not under the 33rd section, but by force of his position as heir to property to which his father was by reason of that section absolutely entitled.

Property comprised in a lapsed devise or bequest falls into the residue if the will contains a residuary clause, and if it does not, goes to the next heir or next of kin, according to whether it is real or personal property.

The student must be careful not to confuse a lapse with the subject of ademption of a legacy. By the ademption of a legacy is meant the failure of a specific legacy by the disposal of the subject matter of it during the testator's lifetime. A mere pledge of the subject of the legacy will not amount to an ademption. There is no ademption of a demonstrative legacy, for if the specified fund ceases to exist, the legacy then takes effect out of the general estate. (And as to the doctrine of ademption or satisfaction, see *post*, pp. 110–113.)

LORD BRAYBROKE v. INSKIP.

(*Lead. Cas. Conv.* 986.)

(8 *Ves.* 417.)

Decided :—That by a devise in general terms a trust estate will pass, unless an intention to the contrary can be inferred from expressions in the will, or the purposes or objects of the testator.

Note.—This decision, though in its direct effect now almost obsolete by reason of the enactment previously mentioned, must yet be carefully studied to understand such enactment. It may be taken as establishing the rule, not only as to ordinary trust estates, but also as to mortgaged estates, and with regard to what would amount to a contrary intention, so that thereby trust and mortgaged estates would not pass, if a testator charged the property comprised in the residuary devise with debts, legacies, or annuities, or otherwise, or subjected his residuary estate to a series of complicated limitations, this being incompatible, and inconsistent with his duties or powers in dealing with either trust or mortgaged estates was held to shew a contrary intention and prevent the trust or mortgaged estates passing,

A constructive trust was held to pass equally with an express trust under a general devise, provided there was no contrary intention ; and it was also decided that under a general devise of *trust* estates an estate of which testator is only constructive trustee would pass (*Lysaght* v. *Edwards*, L. R. 2 Ch. D. 499). In that case the facts were as follows :—In 1874 the plaintiffs entered into a contract for the purchase of real estate. After the title had been accepted and before completion the vendor died, having by his will dated in 1873 given his personal estate to E., whom he appointed executor, and devised all his real estate to H. and M., upon trust for sale, and having also devised to H. alone all the real estate which at his death might be vested in him as trustee. It was held by Jessel, M.R., that the vendor was a constructive trustee of the estate he had contracted to sell, and that it passed to H. under the devise of trust estates.

The above is still the law in the case of deaths prior to January 1, 1882; but with regard to deaths on or since that date, sections 4 and 30 of the Conveyancing Act, 1881 (44 & 45 Vict. c. 41), altogether alter the position. Section 30, dealing with the whole subject of trust and mortgaged estates generally, enacts that any such estates vested solely in any person shall, *notwithstanding any testamentary disposition*, vest absolutely in his personal representatives, so that any devise of trust and mortgaged estates is superfluous and of no effect. This would appear to comprise all cases not only of mortgaged estates and express trust estates, but also constructive trust estates, so as to govern such a case as that of *Lysaght* v. *Edwards;* but in addition, section 4 enacts that where at the death of any person there is subsisting a contract enforceable against his heir or devisee, for the sale of a fee simple or other freehold interest descendible to his heirs general in any land, his personal representatives shall have power to convey the land, for all the estate and interest vested in him at his death, in any manner proper for giving effect to the contract.

PAWLETT v. PAWLETT.

(*Lead. Cas. Conv.* 816.)

(1 *Vern.* 321.)

Lord Pawlett, by settlement, limited certain lands for the purpose (amongst other things) of raising portions for younger children, payable at twenty-one or marriage. One of the daughters died under twenty-one, and unmarried, and her administratrix instituted this suit to obtain payment of her portion.

Decided :—That her portion should not be raised for the benefit of her administratrix, though it would have been otherwise in the case of a legacy.

STAPLETON v. CHEALES.

(*Lead. Cas. Conv.* 820.)

(*Prec. Chan.* 17.)

Decided :—(1) That if a legacy is bequeathed to an infant " payable" or " to be paid " at the age of twenty-one years, it is a vested interest, the time of payment only being postponed, so that it shall go to the personal representatives of the infant, though he dies before that age.

(2) But if a legacy is bequeathed to an infant " at " twenty-one, or " if" or " when" he shall attain the age of twenty-one, this is a contingency, and if the legatee dies before the appointed age the legacy is lapsed and shall not go to the personal representatives, *unless interest is given in the meantime.*

HANSON v. GRAHAM.

(*Lead. Cas. Conv.* 822.)
(6 *Ves.* 239.)

Decided :—That the word " when " standing alone and unqualified in a will is conditional ; but that it may be controlled by expressions and circumstances, so as to postpone *not* the vesting but the payment only, as where the interest of the legacy in the intervals is directed to be laid out at the discretion of the executors for the benefit of the legatees.

Notes on these three Cases.—" The result of the question whether a gift is vested or contingent is most important; because in the former case, although the devisee or legatee die before the event happens which gives him actual possession or enjoyment, the property devised or bequeathed becomes transmissible to his representatives; whilst, on the other hand, if the gift be contingent upon the happening of a certain event which never takes place, the property will go to others." (Lead. Cas. Conv. 832.)

The case of *Pawlett* v. *Pawlett* goes to shew that when the party to be benefited dies, a portion shall not be raised, though a legacy under similar circumstances would ; while the two latter cases shew when it is that a legacy will be considered an actually vested interest, with payment only postponed, and when it will be but a contingency.

The circumstance that a legacy is given for some particular purpose does not render it contingent; thus if a legacy is given to an infant to apprentice him, and he dies before he is apprenticed, his representatives will still get the legacy.

MORLEY v. BIRD.

(Lead. Cas. Conv. 876.)

(3 *Ves.* 629.)

Decided :—That notwithstanding the leaning of the Court to a tenancy in common, in preference to a joint tenancy, an interest simply given to two or more, either by way of legacy or otherwise, is joint, unless there are words of severance, as " equally among," or words to the like effect, or unless an inference of that sort arises in Equity from the nature of the transaction, as in partnership, &c.

LAKE v. GIBSON.
LAKE v. CRADDOCK.

(1 *Lead. Cas. Eq.* 198.)

(1 *Eq. Cas. Ab.* 294, *pl.* 3.)

Here five persons purchased West Thorock Level from the commissioners of the sewers, and the conveyance was to them as joint tenants in fee, but they contributed rateably to the purchase, which was to the intent of draining the level. Several of them died.

Decided :—That they were tenants in common in Equity, for the purchase was for the purpose of a joint undertaking; and though one of these five persons deserted the partnership for thirty years, yet he was afterwards let in on terms.

Notes on these Cases.—The rule at law with regard to two or more persons taking property has always been that they are joint tenants, the maxim being *Jus accrescendi præfertur ultimæ voluntatis*, except indeed in the case of merchants, where there has always been an exception to the rule of survivorship, for *Jus accrescendi inter mercatores pro beneficio commercii locum non habet*.

The above case of *Morley* v. *Bird* decides that where property is given to several without anything else, that must be a joint tenancy ; and *Lake* v. *Gibson* and *Lake* v. *Craddock* shew the leaning of Equity to a tenancy in common, and that a purchase for a joint undertaking, though the conveyance be to the parties as joint tenants, will constitute a tenancy in common ; and this decision forcibly illustrates the maxim, "Equality is equity." Although, if persons purchase an estate and pay equal portions of the purchase-money, and take a conveyance in their joint names, this is a joint tenancy (unless for the purpose of some joint undertaking), yet if the purchase-money is paid in unequal proportions, there will be no survivorship, but they hold the estate in proportion to the sum which each advanced : and in the case of a mortgage to two or more jointly, even though the money is advanced equally, there is no survivorship, but the survivor or survivors will be a trustee or trustees for the personal representatives of the deceased. To prevent the application of this rule it has been the practice when two or more trustees advance money on mortgage to insert a declaration in the deed that the money is advanced on a joint account, and that the receipt of the survivor shall be a sufficient discharge; for in this case it would be very inconvenient for the representatives of a deceased trustee to have an interest and to be necessary parties in reconveying when the mortgage money is paid off. Although in practice this declaration appears to be still inserted in such mortgages, yet there is strictly now no need for it, as by sect. 61 of the Conveyancing Act, 1881 (44 & 45 Vict. c. 41), it is provided that where a mortgage is made to two or more persons jointly, and not in shares, the mortgage money shall be deemed to belong to them on a joint account as between

them and the mortgagor, and the receipt of the survivor shall
be a sufficient discharge, notwithstanding any notice to the
payer of a severance of the joint account. This provision,
however, only applies to mortgages made on or since 1st January,
1882. The purchase by joint mortgagees of the equity of
redemption is unlike an ordinary joint purchase, for they will in
Equity still be tenants in common, because the purchase is
founded on the mortgage.

Notwithstanding the leaning of Equity to a tenancy in common as giving really the true equality, yet if property, instead
of having been *purchased* for a partnership, has been devised to
the partners as joint tenants, and used by them for partnership
purposes, they will still be joint tenants, and not tenants in
common, unless by express agreement, or by their course of
dealing with it for a long period, an intention to sever the joint
tenancy may be inferred (1 Lead. Cas. Eq. 212).

In those cases in which Equity considers a tenancy in common
to be created the survivor is treated as a trustee for the representatives of the deceased person, an implied trust being created,
founded upon an unexpressed but presumable intention.

LORD GLENORCHY v. BOSVILLE.

(1 *Lead. Cas. Eq.* 1.)
(*Cas. temp. Talbot*, 3.)

Here Sir Thomas Pershall devised real estates to trustees upon trust, upon the happening of the marriage of his granddaughter Arabella Pershall, to convey the said estates with all convenient speed to the use of the said Arabella Pershall for life, remainder to husband for life, remainder to the issue of her body, with remainder over.

Decided :—That though Arabella Pershall would have taken an estate tail had it been the case of an immediate devise, yet that the trust, being executory, was to be executed in a more careful and accurate manner, and that a conveyance to Arabella Pershall for life, remainder to her husband for life, with remainder to their first and every other son, with remainder to the daughters, would best serve the testator's intent.

Notes.—The above case clearly shews the distinction between executed and executory trusts. In Snell's "Principles of Equity" an executed trust is defined as one "when no act is necessary to be done to give effect to it, the trust being finally declared by the instrument creating it," and an executory trust as "a trust raised either by stipulation or direction in express terms, or by necessary implication to make a settlement or assurance to uses or upon trusts which are indicated in, but do not appear to be finally declared by, the instrument containing such stipulation or direction." The distinction between these two kinds of trusts forms the best illustration that can be given of the true meaning of the maxim, " Equity follows the

Law ;" for as regards an executed trust, the same construction
will be put on it in Equity as at Law ; but as regards an executory trust, only where an analogy plainly subsists, and there
is no equitable reason to deviate from the rule.

A very material distinction should here be noted between
trusts executory in marriage articles and trusts executory in
wills; for in the former, from the nature of the transaction, the
intention of the parties can always be presumed, whilst in the
latter it can only be gathered from the words used in the will :
and therefore in wills very frequently a construction must be
put on such a trust according to the literal meaning, because
there is nothing to guide one to any other construction, though
if the same words had been used in marriage articles, the construction would have been different, the object of the marriage
articles forming a guide to the intention. Thus, if in marriage
articles an estate is limited to the husband and the heirs of his
body, the Court will yet construe this as only giving a life estate
to the husband and an estate tail to the first and other sons,
because marriage articles are naturally intended as a provision
for the children of the marriage, and to give the husband an
estate tail would be to frustrate the very objects of the articles,
because he might at once bar it.   But in the case of a like provision in a will, although in the nature of an executory trust,
the husband will take an estate tail, unless some intention can
be found from the words used in the will, that he is only to
take a life estate, for there is nothing from the nature of the
instrument like there is in the case of marriage articles to shew
that he was only intended to take a life estate.

With regard to marriage articles it may be observed, that
where there are articles entered into before marriage, and after
marriage a settlement is executed, the articles govern; but
where both the articles and the settlement are made before the
marriage, the parties are concluded by the settlement, unless it
recites that it is made in pursuance of the articles, when it will
be made subservient to them (see *Legg* v. *Goldwire*, 1 Lead.
Cas. Eq. 17.

ELLISON v. ELLISON.

(1 *Lead. Cas. Eq.* 273.)

(6 *Ves.* 656.)

Decided :—That there is this distinction as to volunteers, viz. : The assistance of the Court cannot be had without consideration, to constitute a party *cestui que trust* as upon a mere voluntary covenant to transfer stock, &c. ; but if the legal conveyance is *actually made* constituting the relation of trustee and *cestui que trust*, as if the stock is actually transferred, &c., though without consideration, the equitable interest will be enforced.

Notes.—Where a settlor actually constitutes himself a trustee for volunteers, a Court of Equity will enforce the trusts declared; and such cases as these must be carefully distinguished from those in which it is intended to confer upon persons the whole interest without trustees; thus, if a person disposes of property informally in favour of a volunteer, *no* assistance will be given in Equity, but if he simply declares himself to be a trustee of that property, a complete trust is created, and the Court will act upon it.

An instance of an informal attempt to dispose of an interest is found in the case of *Antrobus* v. *Smith* (12 Ves. 39). In that case one Crawford made the following indorsement upon a receipt for one of the subscriptions in the Forth and Clyde Navigation : " I do hereby assign to my daughter Anna Crawford all my right, title and interest of and in the enclosed call and all other calls of my subscription in the Clyde and Forth Navigation." This was no complete legal assignment, but it was attempted to be argued that the father meant to make himself a trustee for his daughter of these shares. It was, however, held that there was no trust created, the Master of the Rolls saying, " Mr. Crawford

E

was no otherwise a trustee than as any man may be called so who professes to give property by an instrument incapable of conveying it. He was not in form declared a trustee, nor was that mode of doing what he proposed in his contemplation. *He meant a gift.* He says he assigns the property. But it was a gift not complete. The property was not transferred by the act. Could he himself have been compelled to give effect to the gift by making an assignment? There is no case in which a party has been compelled to perfect a gift, which in the mode of making it he has left imperfect. There is a *locus pœnitentiœ* as long as it is incomplete."

A somewhat recent case on this subject is that of *Richards* v. *Delbridge,* L. R. 18 Eq. 686, in which Jessel, M.R., held that certain words professing to make a gift (which was an imperfect gift) constituted no valid declaration of trust. The following portion of his Lordship's judgment seems especially useful :—" The principle is a very clear one. A man may transfer his property without valuable consideration in one of two ways : he may either do such acts as amount in law to a conveyance or assignment of the property, and thus completely divest himself of the legal ownership, in which case the person who by those acts acquires the property takes it beneficially, or on trust as the case may be ; or the legal owner of the property may by one or other of the modes recognized as amounting to a valid declaration of trust, constitute himself a trustee, and without an actual transfer of the legal title, may so deal with the property as to deprive himself of its beneficial ownership, and declare that he will hold it from that time forward on trust for the other person. It is true he need not use the words, 'I declare myself a trustee,' but he must do something which is equivalent to it, and use expressions which have that meaning ; for however anxious the Court may be to carry out a man's intention, it is not at liberty to construe words otherwise than according to their proper meaning. . . . . The true distinction appears to me to be plain and beyond dispute ; for a man to make himself a trustee, there must be an expression of intention to become a trustee, whereas words of present gift shew an intention to give over property to another, and not to retain it in the donor's own hands for any purpose, fiduciary or otherwise."

In the absence of an express power of revocation a conveyance or a declaration of trust in favour of a volunteer *cannot* be revoked or avoided, *except* that in the case of an assignment of property in favour of creditors it is revocable until the creditors have assented to the trust, and this whether they are individually named or not.

It must be borne in mind that although, as decided in the above case, Equity will not enforce any executory trust raised by covenant or agreement unless there is a valuable consideration, yet that this does not apply to executory trusts arising under wills, for those will be carried out. (See further on the subject of the principal case and the notes, Snell's Principles of Equity, 6th ed., 63-73.)

If application is made to the Court to set aside some voluntary instrument on the ground of fraud, the onus lies on the defendant to prove that such voluntary instrument was fairly and honestly made, without any fraud or pressure upon his part; and if he stood in a fiduciary capacity towards the persons making such voluntary instrument, he must, in addition, shew how the intention to make it was produced in the other person (Indermaur's Princ. of the Com. Law, 3rd ed. 451).

FOX v. MACKRETH.

(*Lead. Cas. Eq.* 123.)
(2 *Cox*, 320.)

In this case the defendant Mackreth, being a trustee for the plaintiff Fox of certain property, agreed to buy such property of him for a sum of £39,500, and such agreement was duly carried out by conveyances being subsequently executed. Mackreth immediately afterwards sold the property to a Mr. Page for £50,500, and the plaintiff discovering this, filed his bill to have advantage of it.

Decided :—That Mackreth having purchased the estate from his *cestui que trust* while the relation of trustee and *cestui que trust* continued to subsist between them, and without having communicated to the plaintiff the value of the estate acquired by him as trustee, he must be and was declared a constructive trustee as to the sum produced by the sale to Mr. Page.

Notes.—The true ground of the above decision was *not* the under-value, but as stated above; but it must be noted that a trustee can purchase from a *cestui que trust* who is *sui juris*, and has discharged him from all the obligations which attached to him as trustee; but even then any such transaction will be viewed by the Court with jealousy, and the trustee must shew that there is a clear and distinct contract, ascertained to be such, after the fullest examination of all the circumstances, that the *cestui que trust* intended the trustee should buy, and that there is no fraud, concealment, or possible advantage taken by the trustee of any information acquired by him in his character of trustee. (See hereon, Snell's Princ. of Eq. 6th ed. 469.)

Practically the only safe way for a trustee to buy is by leave of the Court on application, shewing the full particulars and the advantage to the *cestuis que trusts*. Such an application must now be made by an originating summons in Chambers under Order lv. Rule 3. (See Indermaur's Manual of Practice, 3rd ed. 218, 219.)

KEECH v. SANDFORD.

(1 *Lead. Cas. Eq.* 46.)

(*Select Cas. in Chancery,* 61.)

Here the lease of Rumford Market had been bequeathed to B. in trust for an infant. B. before the expiration of the term applied to the lessor for a renewal of the lease for the benefit of the infant, and this was refused. B. then got a lease made to himself. On this suit being brought by the infant to have the lease assigned to him—

Decided:—That B. was a trustee of the lease for the infant, and must assign the same to him.

ROBINSON v. PETT.

(2 *Lead. Cas. Eq.* 207.)

(3 *P. Wms.* 132.)

Decided:—That the Court never allows an executor or trustee for his time and trouble; neither will it alter the case that the executor renounces, and yet is assisting to the executorship; and this, even though it appears that the executor or trustee has benefited the trust to the prejudice of his own affairs.

Notes on these two Cases.—The above two cases are here placed to immediately follow *Fox* v. *Mackreth,* as although that case certainly bears on a subject that they do not—viz., *purchases* by a trustee—yet they all in common are decisions on the position of a trustee, and go to shew that he can make no profit from his trust. If he does so, he becomes a constructive trustee of that profit for his *cestui que trust*. And this furnishes a good instance of a constructive as opposed to an implied trust (as to which see *Dyer* v. *Dyer*, *post*, p. 63), for the trust is raised here to satisfy the demands of justice without reference to any presumable intention of the parties. A fair contract between trustees or executors and their *cestuis que trust* who are *sui juris* to receive some compensation for acting is, however, good, and trustees and guardians managing the estates of West India proprietors, are entitled to a commission not above £6 per cent. so long as they personally take care of the management and improvement of the estates committed to their charge; but not if they leave the island and trust the management to others acting as attorneys (2 Lead. Cas. Eq. 213). An executor appointed in the East Indies was formerly entitled to a commission of £5 per cent. upon the receipts or payments, but this is not so now, unless expressly given him by the testator (Ibid. 214).

Where an executor or trustee is a solicitor, the right course is to expressly authorize him by the trust instrument to make his proper professional charges, and if he is so authorized he is entitled to do so; but even here he is only allowed for strict professional duties, and would not be allowed to charge for doing acts which a trustee or executor would ordinarily do personally without employing a solicitor. If a solicitor is appointed trustee without the proper provision being made for his charges, the rule is just the same as if he were a private person, viz., that he can charge nothing but reasonable expenses out of pocket. However, it has been decided that where a trustee is a solicitor, he may be employed by his *cestuis que trust* or co-trustees in an action relating to the trust affairs, and make the usual charges if this does not increase the costs (*Cradock* v. *Piper*, 15 L. T. Rep. 61); but this case has not been approved of, and is not to be at all extended, and does not apply where the trustee acts for himself and his co-trustee in the administration of the trust estate out of Court (2 Lead. Cas. Eq. 212).

It may not be out of place to give here a short statement of the duties of trustees with regard to the investment of trust funds under their control, where the instrument under which they are acting does not contain any provisions on the subject.

Before any statute on the subject it would seem they could only invest in £3 per Cent. Annuities.

By 22 & 23 Vict. c. 35, they were allowed to invest in real securities in any part of the United Kingdom, or in stock of the Bank of England or Ireland, or East India stock.

By 23 Vict. c. 38, this provision was made retrospective.

By 30 & 31 Vict. c. 132, it is provided that trustees may invest in any securities the interest of which is guaranteed by Parliament.

By the 34 & 35 Vict. c. 47 (s. 13), it is provided that trustees may invest in Consolidated Stock of the Metropolitan Board of Works.

With regard to capital money arising under the provisions of the Settled Land Act, 1882 (45 & 46 Vict. c. 38), that may, under section 21, be applied not only on such investments as before mentioned, but also on the security of bonds, mortgages, or debentures, or in the purchase of the debenture stock of any railway company in Great Britain or Ireland incorporated by special Act of Parliament, and having for ten years next before the date of investment paid a dividend on its ordinary stock or shares, or in the discharge of any incumbrance on the settled land, or in the payment for any improvement authorized by the Act (see sect. 25), or in the purchase of lands in fee simple, or of leaseholds having not more than 60 years to run.

It has also been provided by the Debenture Stock Act, 1871 (34 & 35 Vict. c. 27, s. 1), that where trustees have a power to invest in the mortgages or bonds of any company, they shall, unless the contrary is expressly declared by the trust instrument, have the power of investing in the debenture stock of such company. And by the Local Loans Act, 1875 (38 & 39 Vict. c. 83, s. 27) it is also provided that any trustees authorized to invest in debentures or in debenture stock of any company shall, unless the contrary is expressly declared by the trust instrument, have the power of investing in any debenture stock issued under the provisions of that Act.

By the East India Loan (East India Railway Debentures) Act, 1880 (43 Vict. c. 10), power is given to the Secretary of State to raise in the United Kingdom, for the service of the Government of India, certain moneys by the creation and issue of bonds, debentures, or capital stock (sect. 1), and it is provided that any capital stock so created is to be deemed East India Stock within 22 & 23 Vict. c. 35.

As to the amount trustees may safely advance, the strict rule seems to be, that they should not advance more than two-thirds of the value of agricultural freeholds, or more than one-half the value of houses, but this is not a hard and fast rule, and is not enforceable with exact strictness (*In re Godfrey, Godfrey* v. *Faulkner*, L. R. 23 Ch. D. 483).

If a trustee neglects to make the proper investments that he should have made, the claim of the *cestui que trust* against him is ordinarily for the principal money and interest at £4 per cent. per annum from the time at which it ought to have been invested. If, however, the trustees are specially prohibited from investing in anything except £3 per Cents. then they are liable for the amount of £3 per Cents. which would have been produced by a conversion and investment at the proper time, together with interest at £3 per cent. per annum on the same amount from that time (Prideaux's Conveyancing, 12th ed. vol. ii. 401). A trustee may, however, be liable for more than just stated under exceptional circumstances, which have been stated to be as follows :—

1. Where he ought to have received more, as when he had improperly called in a mortgage carrying 5 per cent.

2. Where he has actually received more than 4 per cent.

3. Where he must be presumed to have received more than 4 per cent., as if he has traded with the money, in which case the *cestui que trust* has it at his option to take the profits actually obtained ; and

4. Where the trustee is guilty of direct breaches of trust or gross misconduct (Snell's P'pls. of Eq. 6th ed. 160).

HUGUENIN v. BASELEY.

(2 *Lead. Cas. Eq.* 547.)
(14 *Ves.* 273.)

Here the plaintiff, Mrs. Huguenin, whilst a widow, constituted the defendant her agent, and he undertook the management of her property and affairs; and she afterwards executed a voluntary settlement in favour of him and his family. Mrs. Huguenin having now married, this suit was brought by her and her husband for the purpose of setting aside the settlement.

Decided :—That the settlement should be set aside as obtained by undue influence and abused confidence in the defendant as an agent undertaking the management of her affairs; upon the principles of public policy and utility, applicable to the relation of guardian and ward.

Notes.—The above case forms an instance of a constructive fraud, and proceeds upon the ground of the confidential relation existing between the parties; for it is a rule, that when any such confidence exists, and the party in whom it is reposed makes use of it to obtain an advantage to himself at the expense of the party confiding, he will never be allowed to retain any such advantage, however unimpeachable such transaction would have been if no such confidence had existed. This is upon general principles of public policy.

The rules of Equity in relation to gifts *inter vivos*, by which fraud is presumed when they are obtained from persons standing in certain relations to the donors, have been held not applicable to gifts by will (*Parfitt* v. *Lawless*, L. R. 2 P. & D. 462; *Ashwell* v. *Lomi*, L. R. 2 P. & D. 477. See, however, hereon 2 Lead. Cas. Eq. 589).

ELLIOTT v. MERRYMAN.

(1 *Lead. Cas. Eq.* 64.)

(*Barnardiston's Chan. Reps.*)

Decided : — 1. That where real estate is devised to
trustees upon trust to sell for payment of debts generally,
or charged with payment of debts, the purchaser is *not*
bound to see that the money is rightly applied ; but if
the real estate is devised upon trust to be sold for the
payment of certain debts, mentioning to whom in particular those debts are owing, the purchaser is bound to
see that the money is applied in payment of those debts.

2. But that a purchaser of leasehold or other personal
estate is never liable to see to the application of the purchase-money—except in cases of fraud—because the executors are the proper persons that by law have the power
to dispose of a testator's personal estate.

Notes.—It is now enacted by 22 & 23 Vict. c. 35, s. 23, as
follows :—" The *bonâ fide* payment to, and the receipt of, any
person to whom any *purchase or mortgage money* shall be payable
upon any express or implied trust, shall effectually discharge
the person paying the same from seeing to the application or
being answerable for the misapplication thereof, unless the contrary shall be expressly declared by the instrument creating the
trust or security." It is also enacted by the Conveyancing Act,
1881 (44 & 45 Vict. c. 41, s. 36), in substitution for 23 & 24
Vict. c. 145, s. 29, which is repealed by s. 71, that with regard
to trusts created either before or after the commencement of the
Act, " the receipt in writing of any trustees or trustee for any
money, securities, or other personal property or effects payable,
transferable, or deliverable to them or him under any trust or

power, shall be a sufficient discharge for the same, and shall
effectually exonerate the person paying, transferring, or delivering the same from seeing to the application or being answerable
for any loss or misapplication thereof."

This latter Act is more extensive than the former, which in
fact may be considered as practically merged in it. By reason also
of the provisions of the two statutes, the above case is of much
less importance than formerly. (As to trustees' receipts generally,
see Lewin on Trusts, ch. 18, s. 2 ; and Dart's Vendors and
Purchasers, ch. 13, s. 3.)

With regard to the power of executors and trustees to accept
compositions, take security, &c., see s. 37 of the Conveyancing
Act, 1881.

DERING v. EARL OF WINCHILSEA.

(1 *Lead. Cas. Eq.* 106.)

(1 *Cox*, 318.)

Here two different bonds had been given to the Crown for the due performance by one Thomas Dering of a certain office, and he becoming in arrear to the Crown, one of the bonds was put in suit, and judgment recovered on it.   This suit was then instituted against those who had given the other bond claiming a contribution.

Decided :—That though the sureties were bound by different instruments, they must contribute, for the doctrine of contribution amongst sureties is not founded in contract, but is the result of general equity, on the ground of equality of burden and benefit.

Notes.—And this right of a surety to enforce contribution against co-sureties will not be affected by his ignorance at the time he became surety that they also were co-sureties.   Courts of Common Law could also compel contribution between sureties ; but there was this important distinction between contribution in Equity and at Common Law : in Equity the contribution was with reference to the time when it was sought to be enforced, but at Common Law with reference to the number of sureties originally liable.   Thus : A., B., and C. being sureties, A. is forced to pay the whole amount.   B. has become insolvent ; nevertheless at Common Law A. could only recover a third from C., though in Equity he could recover half.   Further, if a surety died, contribution could be enforced in Equity as against his representatives ; but at Common Law the surviving sureties only could be sued (see *Batard* v. *Hawes*, 2 Ell. & B. 287).   However, the student will remember that now, under the Judicature Act,

1873 (sect. 25), where the rules of Law and Equity formerly clashed, the rules of Equity now prevail.

With regard to the rights of sureties who are compelled to pay their principal's debt, it is provided by 19 & 20 Vict. c. 97, s. 5, that " every person who being a surety for the debt or duty of another, or being liable with another for any debt or duty, shall pay such debt or perform such duty, shall be entitled to have assigned to him, or a trustee for him, every judgment, specialty, or other security which shall be held by the creditor in respect of such debt or duty, whether such judgment, specialty, or other security shall or shall not be deemed at law to have been satisfied by the payment of the debt or performance of the duty; and such person shall be entitled to stand in the place of the creditor." Before this statute, if the debt was secured by bond or by judgment, and the surety paid the amount, he could not obtain an assignment of the bond or judgment itself, but only of collateral securities. The right to the delivery up of securities held by the creditor extends not only to a direct surety, but also to one who is so merely because of having indorsed a bill of exchange or promissory note (*Duncan Fox & Co. v. North & South Wales Bank*, L. R. 6 App. Cases, 1; 50 L. J. (Ch.) 335).

As to the different ways in which a surety may be discharged, see Indermaur's Princ. of the Com. Law, 3rd ed. 43, 44.

Where one or some of several sureties only is or are sued, with a view of obtaining contribution in that action from the co-surety or co-sureties, he or they may, by means of a "third party notice," be brought in in the existing action and judgment obtained against them (Order xvi. rr. 48–51; Indermaur's Manual of Practice, 3rd ed. 38, 39).

DYER v. DYER.

(1 *Lead. Cas. Eq.* 223.)

(2 *Cox*, 92.)

Here one Simon Dyer paid the purchase-money for certain property, and took the conveyance to himself, his wife Mary, and a son William, jointly. Simon Dyer survived his wife, and then died, devising all his interest in these premises to the plaintiff, who filed his bill against the son William, insisting that as the purchase-money was all paid by Simon Dyer, the son William, the defendant, was but a trustee.

Decided :—That though if no relationship existed there would be a resulting trust in favour of the person paying the purchase-money; yet the circumstance of the nominee being the child of the purchaser operated to rebut the resulting trust, and the defendant took the property beneficially as an advancement from his father.

Notes.—The presumption of advancement does not only arise in favour of a child, but also in favour of a wife; and in some cases it arises when a person has placed himself in *loco parentis* towards some child. And it has been held that a widowed mother is a person standing in such a relation to her child as to raise the presumption in favour of her child (*Sayre* v. *Hughes,* L. R. 5 Eq. 576).

A binding contract to purchase in the joint names of a man and his wife has been held to entitle the wife to the benefit of the purchase as survivor. Thus in *Vance* v. *Vance* (1 Beav. 605), A. B. directed his banker to invest a sum of money in the joint names of himself and his wife, and their broker accord-

ingly made the purchase. A. B. died after the contract but
before the transfer had been completed. It was held that the
wife was entitled to the stock by survivorship. But where a
husband paid money into a bank to an account opened in his
wife's name as a mere agency account for the purpose of convenience, and without any contract or intention to give the wife
any interest in the money, it was held to be the property of the
husband and not of the wife (*Lloyd* v. *Pughe*, L. R. 8 Ch.
App. 88). Where a conveyance is taken in the name of a
stranger, and therefore by equitable presumption a resulting
trust arises, such resulting trust may be rebutted by parol
evidence shewing that the person who paid the purchase-money
really intended that the person in whose name the conveyance
was taken should take the property for his own benefit.

It seems that if a child has already been fully provided for by
his father, this circumstance may rebut the presumption of an
advancement (1 Lead. Cas. Eq. 245, 246 ; and see *Hepworth* v.
Hepworth, L. R. 11 Eq. 10). The presumption of advancement may equally apply in the case of personal estate as in the
case of real—*e.g.*, where a person purchases stock and causes it
to be transferred into the name of his wife or child (1 Lead.
Cas. Eq. 243).

The presumption of advancement may also be rebutted by
evidence of facts shewing the father's intention that the son
should take property purchased in his name as a trustee and
not for his own benefit. Such facts, however, must have taken
place antecedently to or contemporaneously with the purchase,
or else immediately after it, so as to form in fact part of the
same transaction ; but beyond this subsequent facts will not be
admissible in evidence to shew the intention of the father against
the presumption (1 Lead. Cas. Eq. 247, 248 ; and see *Stock* v.
M'Avoy, L. R. 15 Eq. 59). So also the presumption of advancement may be rebutted by evidence of contemporaneous parol
declarations of the father, but not by any of his declarations
made subsequently to the purchase (see hereon *O'Brien* v. *Sheil*,
L. R. 7 Eq. 255).

A *fortiori* parol evidence may be given by the son to shew

the intention of the father to advance him ; for such evidence is in support both of the legal interest of the son and of the equitable presumption (1 Lead. Cas. Eq. 250).

Where a son acts as solicitor for his father, the ordinary presumption in favour of a transaction in the name of the son being a gift is excluded, and the burden of proof is thrown upon the son who acts as solicitor (*Fowkes* v. *Pascoe*, L. R. 10 Ch. App. 352.)

The true principle upon which a person in whose name property is purchased by another is held to be a trustee is an implied intention. All such cases form good instances of an implied trust, which is indeed one founded upon an unexpressed but presumable intention. (For an instance of a constructive trust as opposed to an implied trust, see *ante*, *Keech* v. *Sandford*, *ante*, p. 54.)

MACKRETH v. SYMONS.

(1 *Lead. Cas. Eq.* 324.)

(15 *Ves.* 329.)

Decided:—1. That a vendor's lien for unpaid purchase-money, unless relinquished, exists against all persons except purchasers for valuable consideration without notice having the legal estate.

2. That another security taken and relied on may, according to its nature and the circumstances under which taken, be evidence of relinquishment, but the proof is on the purchaser.

Notes.—A vendor's lien may be defined as that hold or charge on property which a person has who has sold the same, but has not received the purchase-money, or the whole of it. This lien exists even though the deed expresses that the consideration is paid and a receipt is indorsed on it. It must be borne in mind that (as decided in the above case) the taking of a security is only an evidence of relinquishment by the vendor of his lien ; and, as a general rule, the taking of a mere personal security —*e.g.*, a bill of exchange or promissory note—will not deprive the vendor of his lien, unless indeed there was a plain intention to substitute it for the lien, though, if he take a totally distinct and independent security, such as a mortgage, the lien is usually lost (*a*).

It has been the practice not only to have a receipt in the body of a deed, but also indorsed thereon, and if it was not so indorsed thereon, this would amount to constructive notice to any purchaser of the existence of a vendor's lien so as to make him subject to it. This is, however, now no longer so on account of

(*a*) As to vendors' liens in respect of personal property, see Indermaur's Princ. of the Com. Law, 3rd ed. 86, 87.

sects. 54 & 55 of the Conveyancing Act, 1881 (44 & 45 Vict. c. 41), which provide that a receipt either in the body of a deed or indorsed thereon is sufficient in all cases.

The amount of the purchase-money for which a vendor's lien existed was of course payable out of the vendee's general personal estate, but now, in consequence of 30 & 31 Vict. c. 69, s. 2, and 40 & 41 Vict. c. 34, in any such case it is primarily payable out of the land in respect of which it exists. (See further hereon notes to Duke of *Ancaster* v. *Mayer*, *post*, p. 90.)

A vendor's lien is by some writers classified as a constructive trust, and by others as an implied trust. It is not a particularly good instance of either, for whilst it may on the one hand be fairly said to be raised simply by construction of Equity to satisfy the demands of justice, yet on the other hand it seems equally correct to say that it is founded on an implied intention.

BRODIE v. BARRY.

(2 *V. & B.* 127.)

Here property was bequeathed to a person who was testator's heiress to heritable property in Scotland, a disposition of which was made by the will, but in a manner not conformable to the law of Scotland, so that it did not pass under the will, and the question was whether the heiress should be allowed both to take the benefits given to her by the will and the property—which, being thus informally dealt with, descended to her as heir-at-law—or whether she should be put to her election.

Decided :—That the Scotch heiress could *not* take both the benefits given her by the will and the property, which, being informally dealt with, would descend to her; but that she must elect between them.

COOPER v. COOPER.

(*L. R.* 7 *Eng. & Ir. Apps.* 53.)

The proceeds of an estate being given in trust as one Mrs. Cooper should appoint, she appointed the same to her three sons, her executors, &c., equally, subject to a power of revocation by deed. She never exercised this power of revocation ; but by her will and codicils, treating herself still as having a disposing power over the said property, she gave it absolutely to the eldest of the three sons, and gave other benefits to the children of the second son (he having in the meantime died leaving children), and also to the third son. This suit was brought to compel the third son and the children of the second son to elect between taking under the settlement or under the will and codicils. There was no contention as to the third son, who admitted that he must elect; but the children of the deceased son objected to elect, on the ground that they, taking their parent's interest under the Statute of Distributions as next of kin, their rights were of an undefined and intangible interest, and not the subject of election.

Decided:—That the Statute of Distributions is nothing but a will made by the Legislature for an intestate, and that (subject to the claims of creditors) the title of the next of kin is substantial and complete, and that the rights of these children of the second son were exactly the same as were the rights of the third son, and that they must elect.

Notes on these two Cases.—The doctrine of election is stated, in Snell's Principles of Equity, to originate in inconsistent or alternative donations, and it consists in the choosing by a person between two rights where there is an intention, express or implied, that they shall not both be enjoyed. The above case of *Brodie* v. *Barry* is given here in preference to those of *Noys* v. *Mordaunt* and *Streatfield* v. *Streatfield*, set out in Messrs. White and Tudor's work, as it forms a very simple and striking example of the doctrine. The second case above given—viz., that of *Cooper* v. *Cooper*—is a recent case before the House of Lords, in which the doctrine of election was somewhat generally discussed; and it is important as carrying the doctrine of election a step further, and deciding that persons taking interests under the Statutes of Distributions are subject to the doctrine of election in the same way as those through whom they claim would have been. It also points out, as incidental to this decision, what really the Statute of Distributions is, and what is the nature of the interest of the next of kin under it.

It is important to remember that when a person elects against an instrument—that is, refuses to give up his own property—he does not always absolutely forfeit the benefits given him by it, but only so much thereof as will compensate the disappointed party. Thus, if a testator gives to A. £1,000, and to B. a house of small value to which A. is entitled, and A. refuses to conform to the testator's will, he is only bound to give up so much of the £1,000 as the house is worth, so as to compensate B.

An election need not necessarily be made in express words—it may be implied; but what will amount to an implied election is a question to be determined principally upon the circumstances of each particular case. And any acts to be binding on a person must be done with a knowledge of his rights, and also with the knowledge of the existence of the doctrine of election and of his right to elect.

Where an infant has to elect, in some cases the period of election is deferred until after he comes of age. In other cases there has been a reference to Chambers to inquire what would be most beneficial to the infant, and in others an order has been made for the infant to elect without a reference to Chambers. The practice as to election by married women also varies, it having been sometimes held that there must be an inquiry what is most beneficial for them, whilst in other cases it has been held that married women can elect, at any rate as to real property, by deed acknowledged (Snell's Principles of Equity, 6th ed., 221). Now, however, by force of the Married Women's Property Act, 1882 (45 & 46 Vict. c. 75), with regard to property *coming to* on or since 1st January, 1883, as she is placed in the position ~~coming to her~~ of a *feme sole*, she can of course elect, and there will not be any necessity for a deed acknowledged.

COUNTESS OF STRATHMORE v. BOWES.

(1 *Lead Cas. Eq.* 446.)

(1 *Ves. Jun.* 22.)

Lady Strathmore, during her engagement of marriage with one Mr. Grey, conveyed and assigned her property to trustees for her separate use, with his approbation. Afterwards hearing that defendant Bowes had fought a duel on her account, she married him. Bowes had no notice of the settlement.

Decided :—That a conveyance by a wife, whatsoever may be the circumstances, and even the moment before the marriage, is *primâ facie* good, and becomes bad only upon the imputation of fraud; and that if a woman, in the course of a treaty of marriage with her, makes, without notice to the intended husband, a conveyance of any part of her property, it will be set aside because affected with that fraud; but that this case was different, the settlement indeed being with the sanction of the then intended husband, and so the settlement here was established.

Notes.—A secret conveyance by a woman pending a marriage engagement has been held to be a fraud on the husband's marital rights, although he did not know she had any property.

There appears to be one exception to the general rule laid down in *Countess of Strathmore* v. *Bowes*, and that is in the case of the previous seduction by a man of his intended wife; for it has been held that, as the husband has by his conduct before the marriage put it out of the wife's power to make any stipulation for settlement of her property, retirement being impossible on her part, a secret settlement made by her shall not be set aside (*Taylor* v. *Pugh*, 1 Hare, 608; but see *Downes* v. *Jennings*, 32 Beav. 290).

It was also formerly supposed that another exception existed in the case of a fair settlement by a widow upon her children by a former marriage, but the authorities do not appear to warrant this, and it cannot therefore be considered as an exception, for "it is conceived that a provision for children would not render a settlement valid which without it would be fraudulent; for although in the execution of a settlement, so far as it makes provision for her children, a wife may perform a moral duty towards her children, she has no right to act fraudulently towards her husband; and she can in such circumstances only reconcile all her moral duties by making a proper settlement on her children with the knowledge of her intended husband" (1 Lead. Cas. Eq. 458).

It would appear that the subject-matter of this case, and notes, is materially affected by the Married Women's Property Act, 1882 (45 & 46 Vic. c. 75). By section 2 it is provided that "every woman who marries after the commencement of this Act (1st Jan. 1883) shall be entitled to have and to hold as her separate property, and to dispose of in manner aforesaid, all real and personal property which shall belong to her at the time of marriage." As therefore she can dispose of her property directly she is married, it seems absurd to suppose that she cannot do so pending the engagement of marriage. It is submitted that there cannot now be such a thing as a fraud on a husband's marital rights, for in fact he has no marital rights as regards the woman's property.

LADY ELIBANK v. MONTOLIEU.
(1 *Lead. Cas. Eq.* 464.)
(5 *Ves.* 737.)

Decided :—That a married woman may, by her next friend, maintain a suit in the Court of Chancery to assert her equity to a settlement on herself and children out of property to which she is entitled; and here the settlement on marriage being inadequate, a further settlement decreed in favour of Lady Elibank.

MURRAY v. LORD ELIBANK.
(1 *Lead. Cas. Eq.* 471, 479.)
(10 *Ves.* 84.)

This case arose out of the foregoing one.   After decree in that suit, but before any settlement in pursuance thereof, Lady Elibank died intestate, and this bill was filed by her infant children for the carrying out of the settlement in their favour notwithstanding her death.

Decided :—That the wife obtained by the decree in the suit of *Lady Elibank v. Montolieu* a judgment for the children, liable to be waived if she thought proper; otherwise to be left standing for their benefit at her death.

Notes on these two Cases.—Equity to a settlement is not any right of property in the wife, but simply a right that she has to come to the Court and ask for a settlement on herself and her children (see hereon Snell's Principles of Equity, 6th ed. 373, 374). It must be clearly understood that the equity to a settlement is strictly personal to the wife, and that the children have no independent equity of their own; so that in the case of *Murray* v. *Lord Elibank*, if Lady Elibank had died before decree her children would not have been entitled to any settlement. If the settlement on a woman's marriage is perfectly adequate, no further settlement will be decreed; but when a settlement is decreed, the amount to be settled is *usually and in the absence of special circumstances* one-half of the property. If after marriage a settlement of property is made upon the wife voluntarily in consideration of her equity to a settlement, it is good as against creditors if the Court would, under the circumstances, have decreed one, had application been made to it for the purpose.

The wife's equity to a settlement forms a good example of the maxim, "He who seeks equity must do equity," for it had its origin in that when the husband came to the Court to get his wife's property, the Court would, under this maxim, insist on his making a provision for his wife.

With regard to the wife waiving her right to a settlement, this she can always do (unless she is a female ward of the Court married without its sanction), by her examination in open Court; and by 20 & 21 Vict. c. 57, she can by deed acknowledged under the Fines and Recoveries Act, with the concurrence of her husband, release or extinguish her right to a settlement out of any personal estate to which she or her husband in her right may be entitled in possession, under any instrument made after the 31st of December, 1857. This Act makes no provision enabling the wife to waive her right in respect of personal estate derived under an intestacy. The wife may also lose her right to a settlement by eloping and living in adultery, unless she is a ward of Court married without its sanction.

And this right generally only exists out of the wife's absolute equitable interests in pure personalty and her absolute equitable interests in leaseholds; but if the husband is not living with and maintaining her, then it exists also out of her life interests in like property, and her life interests in equitable real estate.

The subject-matter of this case and notes will soon cease to be of much practical importance, by reason of the provisions of the Married Women's Property Act, 1882 (45 & 46 Vict. c. 75), that statute providing (sects. 2 and 5) that with regard to women married either before or since its commencement, all real and personal property her title to which accrues after the commencement thereof (1st Jan. 1883), shall be held and disposed of by her as her separate estate.   There will therefore be no occasion to come to the Court to enforce Equity to a settlement when the property is already absolutely the wife's.   Still, at the present time there may be many cases in which the title to property has accrued prior to 1883, so that the subject cannot yet by any means be considered obsolete.

HULME v. TENANT.

(1 *Lead. Cas. Eq.* 521.)
(1 *Bro. C. C.* 16.)

This bill was filed by the obligee of a bond entered into by the defendants (husband and wife) against the husband and wife, and her surviving trustee, to recover the sums secured out of the wife's separate estate.

Decided :—That the bond of a married woman jointly with her husband shall bind her separate property.

HUNTINGDON v. HUNTINGDON.

(2 *Lead Cas. Eq.* 1032.)
(2 *Bro. P. C.* 1, *Toml. Edit.*)

Here the Countess of Huntingdon joined with her husband, the Earl, in a mortgage of her estate of inheritance, for his purposes, and the Earl covenanted to pay the money. He did pay the money, but took an assignment to himself. The mortgage being for a term of years, the Earl devised it for the benefit of his younger children. The Countess died, and also the Earl, and the eldest son filed a bill claiming as heir to the Countess to have the estate freed from the mortgage and the claims of the younger children.

Decided :—That he was so entitled, as the wife's estate was but as surety.

TULLETT v. ARMSTRONG.

(1 *Beav.* 1.)

Here a testator gave certain property to trustees in trust for his wife for life, with remainder to the defendant Mrs. Armstrong (then unmarried) for life in such manner *that it should not be anticipated,* and that no husband should acquire any control over it, and the questions were as to the effect of a gift to the separate use of a woman unmarried at the time, and the effect of the clause against anticipation.

Decided :—That both the separate use clause and the restriction against alienation became effectual on the subsequent marriage, and that such a restraint against alienation is annexed to the separate estate only, and the separate estate has its existence only during coverture, but that whilst the woman is discovert the separate estate, whether modified by restraint or not, is suspended, and has no operation, though it is capable of arising upon the happening of a marriage.

Notes on these three Cases.—Although the separate estate of a married woman may frequently be made liable for her debts, as shewn in *Hulme v. Tennant,* yet no personal decree could formerly be made against her; but this is no longer so, as by the Married Women's Property Act, 1882 (45 & 46 Vict. c. 75), sect. 1, she is made liable as a *feme sole,* and capable of being sued as such, although the liability is only to the extent of the separate estate. With regard to what debts of a married woman her estate was liable for, the general rule has hitherto been that unless restrained from anticipation it would be liable for "all debts, &c., which she expressly charges, or which, judging from the nature thereof, it may be fairly inferred that she intended to charge on her separate estate." Thus, a promissory note signed by her would bind it; and if she of her own accord employed a solicitor, it would be liable for his charges. However, the Married Women's Property Act, 1882 (sect. 1), materially extends this rule in enacting that "every contract entered into by a married woman shall be deemed to be a contract entered into by her with respect to and to bind her separate property, unless the contrary be shewn."

Notwithstanding that the separate estate of a married woman may be liable for her debts, it was held before the Married Women's Property Act, 1882, that she could not be made a bankrupt, even though she was possessed of separate estate (*Ex parte Jones, In re Grissell*, L. R. 12 Ch. D. 484); but that statute (sect. 1) now provides that every married woman *carrying on a trade* separately from her husband, shall in respect of her separate property be subject to the Bankruptcy Laws in the same way as if she were a *feme sole*.

It was decided in the case of *Pike* v. *Fizgibbon* (L. R. 17 Ch. D. 837; 50 L. J. Ch. 394) that a married woman's debts which bound her separate estate would, however, only bind that separate estate to which she was entitled at the date of entering into the engagement, and which still remained at the date of entering of judgment against it, and not separate estate to which she became entitled after the date of entering into the engagement; but now, under the Married Women's Property Act, 1882 (sect. 1), the contracts of a married woman bind not only her then present, but also all future accruing separate property.

The case of *Huntingdon* v. *Huntingdon* goes to shew that though the wife's separate estate may have been charged, yet when it is but for the purposes of the husband, it is only as surety for him, and he must ultimately discharge the liability, notwithstanding the way in which the estate was dealt with afterwards. Thus, in that case the Earl of Huntingdon, on paying off the money, took an assignment to himself, and yet the heir of the wife was held to be entitled to it.   But that case must be taken with this limitation, or rather addition—viz., that if the wife's intention clearly appears to have been to alter the limitation of the equity of redemption, effect will be given to that intention.   No such intention appeared in that case.

If a married woman lets her husband receive her separate property, it will be usually considered as a gift to him ; but she may distinctly lend money to her husband, and if this is the case it is recoverable by her.   If, however, she lends it to him for his trade or business, and he becomes bankrupt, it is treated as his assets, and the wife can only receive a dividend after all other creditors for value have been satisfied (45 & 46 Vict. c. 75, sect. 3).

Tullett v. *Armstrong* is given above as establishing and plainly shewing the effect of the clause against anticipation which is usually inserted in settlements giving income to a woman for her separate use.   It has, however, now been provided by the Conveyancing Act, 1881 (sect. 39), with regard to judgments or orders made on or after 1st Jan. 1882, that " notwithstanding that a married woman is restrained from anticipation, the Court may, if it thinks fit, where it appears to the Court to be for her benefit, by judgment or order, with her consent, bind her interest in any property."   It seems this section was primarily intended to alter the law as declared in *Robinson* v. *Wheelwright* (6 De G. M. & G. 535), where it was held that the Court could not permit a married woman to alienate her restrained property even to the manifest advantage of her estate (Hood and Challis' Conveyancing Acts, 144).   It may also be noticed that a restraint on anticipation in a settlement does not prevent the exercise by a married woman of any power under the Settled Land Act, 1882 (45 & 46 Vict. c. 38, sect. 61).

EARL OF CHESTERFIELD v. JANSSEN.
(1 *Lead. Cas. Eq.* 592.)
(2 *Ves.* 125.)

In this case one Mr. Spencer, at the age of 30, had borrowed £5,000 of defendant on the terms of paying £10,000 if he survived his grandmother, from whom he had large expectations, and who was then of the age of 78 years, and nothing if he did not. He did survive her, and after her death gave a bond for payment of the £10,000, and paid a part. Mr. Spencer having since died, his executor brought this suit to be relieved against this contract as usurious and unconscionable.

Decided :—Not usurious, and (without deciding whether relief would have been given against the original transaction) no relief could now be given, Mr. Spencer having by his acts after his grandmother's death ratified the transaction.

EARL OF AYLESFORD v. MORRIS.
(*Law Rep.* 8 *Ch. App.* 484.)

Here the plaintiff, soon after he came of age, and whilst his father was living, borrowed from the defendant, who was a money-lender, sums amounting to about £7,000, for which he gave bills, which, with interest and discount, together exceeded 60 per cent. These bills were renewed, and after the death of plaintiff's father, defendant sued plaintiff on the bills, and this suit was brought for an injunction to restrain the actions on payment by the plaintiff of the sums advanced, and interest at 5 per cent.

Decided :—That the plaintiff was entitled to the relief sought, and that the fact of his being an actual tenant in tail in remainder (as the case was), instead of being merely an expectant heir, made no difference.

Notes on these two Cases.—*Chesterfield* v. *Janssen* is the leading case on that branch of constructive fraud designated in Snell's Principles of Equity as constructive frauds, as being unconscientious or injurious to the rights of third parties. For although in that case no relief was given because of confirmation by Mr. Spencer of the transaction, yet the particular subject of bargains with expectant heirs was there much considered. As to these, the rule in Equity is to set them aside, unless the purchaser can shew that he paid full consideration, or that the bargain being made known to those to whose estate the expectant was hoping to succeed, was approved of by them ; in which latter case there will at any rate be a strong presumption in favour of the *bona fides* of the transaction, though it must not be placed higher than this. The relief thus given to expectant heirs was formerly also given in the case of the sale of remainders and reversions, but it is no longer ; 31 Vict. c. 4, s. 1, enacting that " no purchase, made *bona fide* and without fraud or unfair dealing, of any reversionary interest in real or personal estate, shall hereafter be opened or set aside *merely on the ground of undervalue ;*" and by sect. 2 the word " purchase" used in sect. 1 has an extended meaning.

The case of *Earl of Aylesford* v. *Morris* is a somewhat recent decision on the subject of bargains with expectant heirs ; and whilst the former principles and rules on the subject are confirmed, they seem also to be somewhat extended, for in that case the plaintiff was not simply an expectant heir, but he was an actual tenant in tail in remainder, and yet it was held that this made no difference, and relief was given.

The most recent case on the subject is, however, that of *Nevill* v. *Snelling* (L. R. 15 Ch. D. 679). In this case the plaintiff was the youngest son of a Marquis, who was a large landed proprietor, but he (the plaintiff) *had no property or expectations except such as might be founded on the position of his father.* The defendant had lent him money without any thought of repayment by the borrower from his own personal resources, but on the credit of his *general expectations*, and in the hope of extorting payment from the father to avoid the exposure attendant on the son's being made a bankrupt. Relief was given by the Court, Mr. Justice Denman holding that the principle on which Equity has granted relief from an unconscionable bargain entered into with an expectant heir or reversioner for the loan of money, applied equally to the case of such a transaction as this, though the plaintiff was not an expectant in the strict sense of the term. (See also hereon an article by the author in the Law Students' Journal, 1st Sept. 1880, p. 125.)

The Infants' Relief Act, 1874 (37 & 38 Vict. c. 62), may here be noticed, as it might possibly sometimes affect cases of bargains with expectant heirs. It provides that all contracts made with infants, except for necessaries, shall be absolutely void, and that no action shall ever be brought upon a ratification of an infant's contract.

MARSH v. LEE.

(1 *Lead. Cas. Eq.* 659.)

(2 *Ventris*, 337.)

Decided :—That if a third mortgagee having advanced his money, *without notice of a second mortgage*, afterwards buy in a first mortgage or statute, yet he (the third mortgagee) having obtained the first mortgage or statute, and having the law on his side and equal equity, he shall thereby squeeze out and gain priority over the second mortgagee.

BRACE v. DUCHESS OF MARLBOROUGH.

(2 *P. Wms.* 491.)

Decided :—That if a judgment creditor, or creditor by statute or recognizance, buys in the first mortgage, he shall *not* tack this to his judgment, &c., and thereby gain a preference, *for he did not advance his money on the immediate credit of the land;* but if a first mortgagee lends a further sum to the mortgagor upon a statute or judgment, he shall retain against a mesne mortgagee till both the mortgage and statute or judgment be paid.

Notes on these two Cases.—In the latter of the above two cases the doctrine of tacking was much considered, and a number of rules on the subject were stated, but the points above set out are the most important to remember in connection with the decision in *Marsh* v. *Lee.* It is very important to know accurately when tacking will be allowed, and when not, and the student will be more likely to remember the distinctions if he bears in mind that tacking is *not* allowed when the money was not originally advanced on the immediate credit of the land.

The doctrine of tacking forms a good illustration of the maxim, "Where the equities are equal the law shall prevail;" for the third mortgagee, being without notice of the intervening incumbrance, has as good a title in conscience as such incumbrancer, and by getting hold of the first mortgage, &c., he has the law on his side.

Tacking was abolished by the Vendors and Purchasers Act, 1874 (37 & 38 Vict. c. 78, s. 7), which section came into operation on the 7th August, 1874; but this provision was repealed by the Land Transfer Act, 1875 (38 & 39 Vict. c. 87, s. 129), except as to anything done thereunder before the commencement of the Act (1st January, 1876).

The student should be careful not to confuse tacking with the doctrine of consolidation of mortgages, which is this, that when the same mortgagor has mortgaged *different* estates to the same mortgagee or to different mortgagees, and they become ultimately vested in one mortgagee, he cannot redeem one of such mortgages without redeeming them all. The cases next given relate to this doctrine.

VINT v. PADGET.

(2 De G. & J. 611.)

Two estates were mortgaged to distinct mortgagees. The mortgagor then made a second mortgage of the two estates to another person. Afterwards the two first mortgages were transferred to one person, with notice of the second mortgage. The transferee then brought a foreclosure suit against the second mortgagee, requiring him to pay off both mortgages.

Decided :—That the transferee was entitled to unite the two mortgages, and that the second mortgagee was not entitled to redeem one without the other.

Notes.—This is the doctrine of consolidation, the distinction between which and tacking is manifest. In this case Lord Justice Turner bases his decision on the ground that the second incumbrancer must be deemed to have taken his security with knowledge that the mortgages in the two estates, though then belonging to different mortgagees, might coalesce and be united against him. The doctrine, however, in its entirety has been much modified. In the case of *Baker* v. *Gray* (L. R. 1 Ch. D. 491), Gray mortgaged property situated in Gray's Inn Lane to three mortgagees successively, each with notice of the other. Gray then mortgaged the same and other property to Baker. Afterwards Baker bought up the first mortgage, and then filed a bill for a declaration that he was entitled to consolidate the first mortgage he had bought up, and his fourth mortgage, as against the two intermediate mortgagees, but it was decided that he had no such right of consolidation.

The limit to be put on the right of consolidation is very clearly put by Vice-Chancellor Hall, in *Baker* v. *Gray* (L. R. 1 Ch. D.

494). He says: "It has been stated that the doctrine depends upon an equity arising out of the right of the mortgagee to say to the person who comes to redeem, 'If you want to redeem you must do equity.' That doctrine is simple enough when the person who wishes to redeem is the mortgagor himself. To him the mortgagee may say, 'You seek to pay me off one mortgage, but I have another debt against you, secured upon another estate, and instead of compelling me to resort to my remedies in respect of such other debt, pay off both mortgages, otherwise you shall not redeem one.' That is intelligible, but when the rights of other persons intervene, it must be seen whether it is or not reasonable to apply this as against them. . . . . There has, however, been no case decided on that principle, applied to the case of a mortgage non-existing at the time when the second mortgage was created."

In a recent case of *Jennings* v. *Jordan* (L. R. 6 App. Cas. 698 ; 51 L. J. Ch. 129), the facts were that a morgagor conveyed the equity of redemption of two cottages to trustees, on the marriage of his daughter, to hold on the trusts of the settlement. The trustees commenced an action against the mortgagee for the redemption of the property. The defendant (who denied all notice of the conveyance to the trustees) sought to consolidate, with the mortgage on the cottages, a mortgage on other property of the mortgagor which had been made subsequently to the conveyance to the trustees. It was decided that the trustees were entitled to redeem the cottages without paying off the charges on the other property. Lord Justice Cotton, in delivering the judgment of the Court, further elucidates the rule that mortgages which were not existent at the time when a third person acquired an interest in the equity of redemption cannot be consolidated. "The principle which allows, as against a subsequent purchaser or mortgagee, the right of consolidation, is, that the mortgagor cannot by any dealing with the equity of redemption prejudice the rights of his mortgagee. This can only apply to rights already given, or arising from acts already done by the mortgagor. The same principle will prevent the mortagor from throwing a greater burden on the purchaser of his equity of redemption, by any act done subsequently to the sale or mortgage of this estate. . . . . In our opinion, the purchaser of an equity of redemption takes subject to such equities as arise from acts previously done by his vendor. . . . . But in our opinion he is not subject to any equity arising from acts done by his vendor subsequently to the sale, and therefore as against a purchaser of an equity of redemption of an estate there can be no consolidation of a mortgage subsequently created on another estate."

The principle of limitation of the doctrine of consolidation has been still further acted upon in the case of *Harter* v. *Colman* (L. R. 19 Ch. D. 630; 51 L. J. Ch. 481). This case decides that when two mortgages, made by the same mortgagor to different mortgagees on different estates, become united for the first time in one person after the mortgagor has assigned (by way either of sale or mortgage) the equity of redemption of one of them, the owner of the two mortgages cannot consolidate them as against the assignee of the equity of redemption, even though both the mortgages were created before the assignment. The assignee of an equity of redemption takes it subject to all equities which affect the assignor in respect of it at the date of the assignment only, but the possibility that the mortgage may by virtue of its subsequent union in the same person with a mortgage of another estate made previously to the assignment by the same mortgagor to a different mortgagee, become liable to consolidation, is not such an equity.

Another recent case that should be noticed in a consideration of this doctrine is that of *Cummins* v. *Fletcher* (L. R. 14 Ch. D. 69; 49 L. J. Ch. App. 563). In that case there were two different mortgages by the same mortgagor to a building society; the property comprised in one of the mortgages, or part of it, was conveyed by the mortgagor to the National Provincial Bank, subject to the one mortgage on it, and the bank duly kept up all payments, but on the other mortgage there was default. The building society sought to consolidate the two properties thus mortgaged to them. The Court held, however, that they were not entitled to do so, for that consolidation only applies where default has been made on all the securities in respect of which it is claimed.

It will be seen from the foregoing observations how much the doctrine of consolidation has been modified, and in addition it has now been provided by the Conveyancing Act, 1881 (44 & 45 Vict. c. 41), sect. 17, with regard to cases in which the mortgages, or one of them, are or is made on or after 1st January, 1882, and so far as no contrary intention is expressed, that a mortgagor seeking to redeem shall be entitled to do so without paying over money due under any separate mortgage made by him, or by any person through whom he claims on property other than that comprised in the mortgage which he seeks to redeem.

BASSETT v. NOSWORTHY.

(2 Lead. Cas. Eq. 1.)
(Rep. temp. Finch, 102.)

This bill was filed by an heir-at-law against a person claiming as purchaser from a devisee under the will of his ancestor to discover a revocation of the will, and the defendant pleaded that he was a purchaser for valuable consideration *bonâ fide,* without notice of any revocation.

Decided :—That this plea was good, and upon proof of it the bill was dismissed.

Notes.—This case proceeded upon the supposition that the plaintiff had a full legal title, and that he might have proceeded at law in an action of ejectment, endeavouring there to make out his case upon his own evidence. The case illustrates the strength which Equity allows to the defence of " *bonâ fide* purchaser for valuable consideration without notice," so that even though the plaintiff had the legal estate, Equity, while exercising its auxiliary jurisdiction (*i.e.,* pure Equity as distinguished from concurrent law), refused to help the plaintiff. This principle is further illustrated by the cases of *Wallwyn* v. *Lee* (9 Ves. 24) and *Heath* v. *Crealock* (L. R. 10 Ch. D. 22).

The principle above enunciated should be carefully considered together with, and distinguished from, the principle embodied in the maxim, " Where the equities are equal, the law shall prevail, as to which see *Marsh* v. *Lee* and notes, *ante*, pp. 83, 84. (See also hereon Snell's Principles of Equity, 6th ed. 23–28.)

DUKE OF ANCASTER v. MAYER.

(1 *Lead. Cas. Eq.* 681.)

(1 *Bro. C. C.* 454.)

Decided :—That the general personal estate is primarily liable to the payment of the debts of the testator, unless exempted by express words or by necessary implication.

Notes.—It may be useful to give here a short statement of, firstly, the order in which assets are applied in payment of debts; and secondly, when the general personal estate is not the primary fund for that purpose.

Firstly. The order is as follows :—

(1) The general personal estate.

(2) Estates devised for the particular purpose of paying debts.

(3) Estates descended.

(4) Property devised or bequeathed to particular devisees or legatees, but charged with payment of debts.

(5) General pecuniary legacies, including annuities, and including also demonstrative legacies which have become general.

(6) Specific legacies (including demonstrative legacies which have remained demonstrative) and real estate devised specifically or by way of residue, and not being at the time charged with debts. (See *Hensman* v. *Fryer*, L. R. 3 Ch. App. 420; *Lancefield* v. *Iggulden*, L. R. 10 Ch. App. 136.)

(7) Property over which the person whose estate is being administered has exercised a general power of appointment by deed to volunteers, or by will.

[handwritten marginal note:] Donationes ~ a liolium? and in ~ or example Country

(8) Paraphernalia of widows. (See Snell's Principles of Equity, 6th ed. 265, 266.)

Secondly. The personal estate is *not* the primary fund for payment of debts in the following cases:—

(1) Where it is exempted by express words.

(2) Where it is exempted by testator's manifest intention : and on this point the fact that the testator has charged his real estate is not alone sufficient, but he must also have shewn that it was his purpose that the personal estate should not be applied.

(3) Where the debt forming the charge or incumbrance is in its own nature real—*e g.*, a jointure.

(4) Where the debt was not contracted by the person whose estate is being administered, but by some one else from whom he or his vendor took it, as in the case of a mortgage created by an ancestor.

(5) In cases coming within the provisions of 17 & 18 Vict. c. 113; 30 & 31 Vict. c. 69; or 40 & 41 Vict. c. 34. (See Snell's Principles of Equity, 6th ed. 266–272.)

As to the order in which debts are paid on a person's decease see Snell's Principles of Equity, 6th ed. 255–264, and particularly observe the effect of 3 & 4 Wm. 4, c. 104; 32 & 33 Vict. c. 46; section 10 of the Judicature Act, 1875; and (with regard to companies) 46 & 47 Vict. c. 28.

RUSSEL v. RUSSEL.

(1 *Lead. Cas. Eq.* 726.)
(1 *Bro. C. C.* 269.)

Here a lease had been pledged with the plaintiff by a person since bankrupt, and the plaintiff now brought his bill against the assignees for a sale of the leasehold estate.

Decided :—That the deposit created a good equitable mortgage.

Notes.—An equitable mortgage by deposit of title-deeds is now of common occurrence, but the above case is cited to show that such a transaction is good, notwithstanding the 4th section of the Statute of Frauds (29 Car. 2, c. 3)—a point which was previously, and with reason, much doubted.

The principle indeed upon which equitable mortgages exist seems to be that they were allowed necessarily from the nature of the case, for a court of law could not assist a person who had pledged his deeds to recover them back, as the answer to such an action would have been that they were pledged, and that the party who pledged them had no right to them until he paid the money; and again, if the person came into equity to recover the deeds, he would have been told, under the maxim, "He who seeks equity must do equity," that he must repay the money before he could have the deeds. (See *per* Lord Abinger in *Keys* v. *Williams*, 3 Y. & C. Exch. Cas. 55, 61.)

The proper remedy of an equitable mortgage by deposit simply is foreclosure (*James* v. *James*, L. R. 16 Eq. 153; 42 L. J. Ch. 386), but if there is a memorandum containing an agreement to execute a legal mortgage, the mortgagee has a right to a sale (*York Union Bank* v. *Artley*, L. R. 11 Ch. D. 205). It would appear that there is nothing in section 25 of the Conveyancing Act, 1881, to alter the correctness of the above distinction (Hood & Challis' Conveyancing Acts, 128).

CUDDEE v. RUTTER.

(1 *Lead. Cas. Eq.* 818.)

(5 *Vin. Ab.* 538, *pl.* 21.)

Decided :—That a bill in Equity will not lie for specific performance of an agreement to transfer a certain sum of South Sea Stock, for there is no difference between that and any other like sum of stock, and no damage occasioned by the non-performance of the agreement specifically, if the difference is paid.

SETON v. SLADE.

(2 *Lead. Cas. Eq.* 501.)

(7 *Ves.* 265.)

Here plaintiff had agreed to sell certain property to defendant, and it was understood that he should make a good title in two months, and defendant gave him a notice that if he did not do so he should insist on the return of his deposit with interest. The plaintiff, however, only delivered his abstract a few days before the expiration of the two months, which the defendant then received and kept without objection.

Decided :—That the vendee upon construction of the circumstances was not entitled to insist on time as of the essence of the contract, and so specific performance decreed.

LESTER v. FOXCROFT.

(1 *Lead. Cas. Eq.* 828.)
(*Colles' P. C.* 108.)

Here a certain *parol* contract had been made for the
pulling down by the plaintiff of certain houses and the
building up of others, and the granting of a lease thereof
to him, and he had, in pursuance and part performance
of such *parol* contract, pulled down the houses and built
some of the others. The plaintiff brought this bill for
specific performance of the contract.

Decided :—That the plaintiff was entitled to a decree
for specific performance, notwithstanding the Statute of
Frauds, because of the acts of part performance by him.

WOOLLAM v. HEARN.

(2 *Lead. Cas. Eq.* 468.)
(7 *Ves.* 211.)

Decided :—That though a defendant resisting specific
performance may go into parol evidence to shew that by
fraud the written agreement does not express the real
terms, a plaintiff cannot do so for the purpose of obtaining specific performance with a variation.

Notes on these four Cases.—These cases are placed together as
relating to the subject of specific performance. *Cuddee* v.
Rutter plainly shews the nature of the contracts of which
specific performance will be granted—viz., those for the breach

whereof damages will not fully compensate; for the idea on which that case proceeded was that practically any quantity of the stock might be had on the market; and it does not apply to shares which are limited in quantity, so that the Court has decreed specific performance of an agreement for the sale of a certain number of shares in a railway company (*Duncroft* v. *Albrecht*, 12 Sim. 199).

The case of *Seton* v. *Slade* shews that though terms may not have been strictly complied with, yet specific performance may be decreed. But in such a case the Court will take care to make proper compensation. And this principle of decreeing specific performance with compensation is applied where the vendor seeks specific performance and has not exactly the interest he contracted to sell, but the difference is not material; but a purchaser cannot be forced to accept lands of a different tenure to what he contracted to buy, for this is not considered a matter for compensation.

The decision in *Lester* v. *Foxcroft* is upon the ground, that after a person has been allowed to do acts in part performance, it would be a fraud on the part of the person who has allowed him to do such acts not to perform his part of the contract. Acts to be a part performance must be exclusively referable to the agreement, and such acts as payment of purchase-money, delivery of abstract, and the like, are *not* sufficient part performance; but letting a purchaser into possession is.

There are also two other cases in which specific performance of a parol contract will be decreed: and they are (1) where it is fully set forth by the plaintiff in his statement of claim, and admitted by the defendant in his statement of defence, and he does not insist on the statute as a bar; and (2) where the agreement was intended to be reduced into writing according to the statute, but that was prevented by the fraud of one of the parties.

With regard to the decision in *Woollam* v. *Hearn*, that a plaintiff cannot get specific performance of a contract with a parol variation, though good as a general rule, yet it must be noted that there are three cases in which a plaintiff may so obtain specific performance with a subsequent parol variation, and they are of a similar nature to the three cases above stated, in which specific performance will be decreed of an original parol contract—viz.: (1) after such acts of part performance of the parol variation; (2) where defendant sets up the parol variation, and plaintiff seeks specific performance with it; and (3) where it has not been put into writing because of fraud. It will be seen that these cases are of an exactly similar nature to those above stated, in which specific performance will be decreed of an original parol contract. The case also shews that a plaintiff cannot generally get specific performance with a parol variation, yet it is always open to a defendant to set up such a variation, the reason being that the Statute of Frauds, although saying that an unwritten agreement as to the sale of land shall not bind, does not say that a written contract shall necessarily bind.

Although by the C. L. P. Act, 1854 (17 & 18 Vict. c. 125), s. 68, a *mandamus* might be awarded at law to compel the performance of certain duties in the fulfilment of which the plaintiff was personally interested, yet it was decided that a person could not be compelled under that Act to perform a contract entered into by him, it only applying to cases of duty arising under a statute or royal charter in which the public as well as the plaintiff are interested (*Benson* v. *Paul*, 25 L. J. Q. B. 274); so that the jurisdiction for obtaining specific performance of a contract still remained exclusively in Equity, and now, under the Judicature Act, 1873, s. 34, the specific performance of contracts is assigned to the Chancery Division of the High Court of Justice.

PUSEY v. PUSEY.

(1 *Lead. Cas. Eq.* 890.)
(1 *Vern.* 273.)

The plaintiff brought this bill for specific delivery up of a certain horn which in ancient times was delivered to his ancestors to hold their land by. The defendant demurred to this bill.

Decided :—That the demurrer must be overruled, and that the heir was well entitled to the horn.

DUKE OF SOMERSET v. COOKSON.

(1 *Lead. Cas. Eq.* 891.)
(3 *P. Wms.* 389.)

The plaintiff, as lord of a certain manor, was entitled as treasure-trove to an old altar-piece made of silver, remarkable for a Greek inscription and dedication to Hercules, and the defendant had obtained possession of the same. This suit was brought to obtain its delivery up in specie undefaced, and the defendant demurred.

Decided :—That this demurrer must be overruled.

Notes on these two Cases.—In the same way that the Court of Chancery has always only decreed specific performance of a contract when it was one for the breach whereof damages would not compensate, so the reason of the above decisions is that the chattel was of such a nature that the loss of it could not be fully compensated for by damages. There is, however, one case in which

II

Equity has always decreed specific delivery of a chattel though of
no peculiar value, and that is where there subsists some fiduciary
relation between the parties.   Specific delivery of a chattel
might, however, to a certain extent, in later times have been
obtained at law, for by the C. L. P. Act, 1854 (17 & 18 Vict. c. 125),
s. 78, the Court might, upon the application of the plaintiff in an
action for the detention of a chattel, order that execution shall
issue for the return of the same without giving the defendant the
option of retaining it upon paying the value assessed; but a
Court of Law under this enactment could only proceed to enforce
the delivery by distringas, whilst a decree in Equity for specific
delivery could always be enforced by attachment.   Also, by the
Mercantile Law Amendment Act, 1856 (19 & 20 Vict. c. 97), s. 2,
the Courts of Law had a further power of this nature given them,
and in cases in which generally Equity would not interfere, for it
is enacted, that on a verdict for plaintiff in an action for breach
of contract, to deliver specific goods for a price of money, on the
application of the plaintiff, and by leave of the judge, the jury
shall find—(1) What are the goods in respect of which the action
is brought; (2) What (if anything) the plaintiff would have been
liable to pay for delivery thereof; (3) What damages (if any)
the plaintiff will be entitled to if the goods are delivered in
execution as thereinafter mentioned; and (4) What damages if
not so delivered.   And thereupon, on the plaintiff's application,
the judge may order execution to be issued *for delivery of the
goods themselves* on payment by the plaintiff of the sum (if
anything) found by the jury to be paid by him, *without giving
the defendant the option of retaining the same* upon paying the
damages assessed.

    It will be observed that the powers given by the two Acts just
mentioned to the Courts of Law were quite irrespective of any
special or peculiar value in the chattel.   Under the Judicature
Act, 1873, it would appear that any division of the High Court
of Justice can give specific delivery of chattels, either under these
Acts or on the principle of special and peculiar value formerly
acted on by the Court of Chancery.

FLETCHER v. ASHBURNER.

(1 *Lead. Cas. Eq.* 896.)

(1 *Bro. C. C.* 497.)

Decided :—That it is an established principle that money directed to be employed in the purchase of land, and land directed to be sold and turned into money, are to be considered as that species of property into which they are directed to be converted; and this, in whatever way the direction is given; and therefore, in this case that real estate having been ordered to be sold, it became personalty, and went accordingly.

ACKROYD v. SMITHSON.

(1 *Lead. Cas. Eq.* 949.)

(1 *Bro. C. C.* 503.)

Here the testator gave several legacies, and ordered his real and personal estate to be sold, his debts and legacies to be paid out of the proceeds arising from the sale, and the residue thereof he gave to certain legatees. Two of these residuary legatees died in the testator's lifetime; and this bill was filed by the next of kin of the testator claiming these lapsed shares, and the question was whether such shares—being originally composed partly of real and partly of personal estate—belonged to the next of kin as being converted into personalty, or

whether the part originally composed of real estate resulted
as real estate, and therefore descended to the heir-at-law
of the testator.

Decided :—That so far as the shares were originally
constituted of personal estate they should go to the next
of kin; but so far as they originally consisted of real
estate they should go to the heir-at-law.

Notes on these two Cases.—"Equity looks on that as done
which ought to be done." It is upon this maxim that the case of
Fletcher v. *Ashburner* proceeds, and that case, or more generally
the whole doctrine of conversion, forms indeed the best illustration of this maxim. Conversion has been well defined as "that
change in the nature of property by which, for certain purposes,
real estate is considered as personal, and personal estate as real,
and transmissible and descendible as such." To effect a conversion it is necessary that the direction to convert be imperative
and *not* optional, and a direction to convert at the request of
certain parties will be held imperative unless it is inserted for
the purpose of giving a discretion to those parties. Conversion
when directed by a deed usually takes place from the date of the
deed, but when directed by a will, from the date of the testator's death. Where
a conversion depends on the exercise of a future option to purchase,
the conversion takes place from the date of the exercise of such
option, and until then the rents and profits go to the persons who
were entitled to the property up to that time. Where a testator
after specifically devising property agrees to sell it, or gives a
person an option of purchasing it which such person exercises,
this operates to substantially revoke the prior devise, but where
he has already agreed to sell it, and then specifically devises
it, the purchase-money takes the place of the estate and goes in
the same way as the estate would have gone (Snell's Principles
of Equity, 6th ed. 179–183).

The case of *Ackroyd* v. *Smithson* is sometimes confused by
students with that of *Fletcher v. Ashburner* as simply deciding

the doctrine of conversion, and they are, chiefly for that reason, considered here together. *Ackroyd v. Smithson* is of course quite beyond the doctrine of conversion, and forms an instance of a resulting trust, shewing that where the purposes of the conversion fail there the property shall remain and go in its original state; thus if a testator devises to trustees to sell and divide the proceeds between two persons, and they die during the testator's lifetime, the property remains in its original state, and if only one of the parties dies, as to his moiety there will be no conversion, but it will go according to its original quality, and the principle of this is, that where an estate is converted merely *for a particular purpose*, and that fails, the Court will not infer an intention to convert for any other purpose. *Ackroyd v. Smithson* is only on the point of a resulting trust in the case of *real* estate directed to be sold, and it was at first doubted whether the rule there established applied to the case of *money* directed to be laid out in the purchase of land to be settled upon trusts which either wholly or partially failed; but it has now long been decided that it does so apply.

Following on the doctrine of Conversion comes that of Reconversion, which has been defined as " that notional or imaginary process by which a prior constructive conversion is annulled and taken away" (Snell's Principles of Equity, 6th ed. 196); thus land is given upon trust to sell and pay the proceeds absolutely to A., and conversion here takes place; but A. can say he prefers the land and will take the land—this is reconversion. If there are several persons interested in the subject-matter the further question arises, Can one reconvert without the consent of the other or others?—that is to say, firstly, land is directed to be sold and the proceeds paid to A. and B.; and secondly, money is directed to be laid out in the purchase of land for A. and B. : in these cases can A. elect to take his share in its original quality; that is, can he reconvert without B.? The answer is, that in the first case he cannot, but in the second he can (Snell's Principles of Equity, 6th ed. 197).

LE NEVE v. LE NEVE.

(2 *Lead. Cas. Eq.* 32.)

(*Amb.* 436.)

Here lands in Middlesex were settled by a deed which was *not* registered. Many years afterwards they were settled on a second marriage, and the settlement was duly registered; but the agent of the person taking the lands under the second settlement had notice of the former.

Decided:—That the object of the Register Act being only to secure subsequent purchasers and mortgagees against *prior secret conveyances* and fraudulent conveyances, the former settlement should be preferred because of the notice, and that notice to an agent or trustee is notice to the principal.

AGRA BANK (Limited) v. BARRY.

(*L. R.* 7 *Eng. & Ir. Apps.* 135.)

In this case one Mr. Barry having borrowed money to a large amount of his wife, who was executrix of her former husband, and being pressed by her to execute some security for the same, consented to give a legal mortgage on certain property of his in Ireland. A solicitor in England was employed to prepare the mort-

gage, and he asked Mr. Barry for the title-deeds, and
Mr. Barry replied that they were at his residence at Lota,
in Cork, and thereupon the mortgage was executed without their production.   It afterwards turned out that the
deeds had been deposited by Mr. Barry with the Agra
Bank by way of equitable mortgage, and the question in
this case was which security should have priority.

Decided :—That the legal mortgage had priority, as
though the absence of the deeds would primarily amount
to constructive notice, yet that constructive notice was
rebutted by the solicitor having inquired for the deeds,
and a reasonable excuse having been given for their non-
production.

Notes on these two Cases.—An interest in property is often rendered subservient to a prior interest by reason of notice, where,
if there had been no such notice, the latter would have had the
preference.   Notice may be either actual or constructive, which
last is, in fact, only evidence of notice the presumption of which
is so violent that the Court will not allow of its being contro-
verted ; and whatever is sufficient to put a person upon inquiry is
constructive notice of everything to which that inquiry might
have led ; thus absence of title-deeds may constitute constructive
notice of some prior interest, but if their absence is satisfactorily
accounted for it will not, as is shewn in the case given above of
the *Agra Bank* v. *Barry.*

It would seem that if a person designedly abstains from
inquiry for the purpose of avoiding notice, he will be affected
with constructive notice notwithstanding.

It should be mentioned that the mere fact of the registration
of a deed affecting lands in a register county is not of itself
notice, so that a prior equitable incumbrance will not, although
registered, affect a subsequent purchaser for valuable consideration without notice who has obtained the legal estate.   It has

also been decided that a further charge is a conveyance requiring registration, and will be void as against a subsequent registered mortgage, not merely postponed to it, so that it cannot be tacked to the first mortgage. (*Credland* v. *Potter*, L. R. 10 Ch. App. 8; 44 L. J. Ch. 169.)   *as to cause in Middlesex ¿ ¿*

Notwithstanding that registration is not of itself notice, when a general search is admitted or proved, then it is a rule of evidence or presumption that the party searching was acquainted with all the contents of the register; but the purchaser may exclude that presumption by shewing that he has confined himself to a more limited search.

It does not necessarily follow that notice to the solicitor of a party is equivalent to notice to him, as there is no such thing as a permanent office of solicitor; and therefore in giving notice it is always desirable to give it direct, or in giving it to a solicitor, to require him to get an acknowledgment from his client, whom it is desired to charge with notice (*Saffron Walden Building Society* v. *Rayner*, L. R. 14 Ch. D. 406).

The Conveyancing Act, 1882 (45 & 46 Vict. c. 39), sect. 3, declares the law as to constructive notice to be as follows:—"A purchaser shall not be prejudicially affected by notice of any instrument, fact, or thing, unless (1) it is within his own knowledge, or would have come to his knowledge if such inquiries and inspections had been made, or ought reasonably to have been made by him; or (2) in the same transaction with respect to which a question of notice to the purchaser arises, it has come to the knowledge of his counsel as such, or of his solicitor or other agent as such, or would have come to the knowledge of his solicitor or other agent as such, if such inquiries and inspection had been made as ought reasonably to have been made by the solicitor or other agent." (See generally on this enactment Hood and Challis' Conveyancing Acts, 193–196.)

With regard to registration under the Middlesex and York-shire Registry Acts (East and North Riding), a will to be valid against subsequent purchasers must be registered within six months after the death of the devisor when he dies in Great Britain, or within three years after the death of the devisor when

he dies on the sea or beyond the seas (7 Ann, c. 20, s. 8;
6 Ann, c. 35, ss. 1, 14; 8 Geo. 2, c. 6, ss. 1, 15). Under the
West Riding Act the will must be registered within six months
if the devisor dies in England, Wales, or Berwick-on-Tweed,
and within three years if he dies elsewhere (2 & 3 Ann, c. 4,
s. 20). It is not necessary to register a will if the devisee is also
heir-at-law, and on the subject of the necessity of registration of
a will the provision of the Vendors and Purchasers Act, 1874
(37 & 38 Vict. c. 78), must now be borne in mind, that Act
enacting (sect. 8) that where the will of a testator devising lands
in Middlesex or Yorkshire has not been registered within the
period allowed by law in that behalf, an assurance of such lands
to a purchaser or mortgagee by the devisee, or by some person
deriving title under him, shall, if registered before, take pre-
cedence of and prevail over any assurance from the testator's
heir-at-law.

HOWE v. EARL OF DARTMOUTH.

(2 *Lead. Cas. Eq.* 296.)

(7 *Ves.* 137.)

Decided :—That it is a general rule that where personal property is bequeathed for life with remainders over, *and not specifically*, it is to be converted into the Three per Cents, subject in the case of a real security to an inquiry whether it will be for the benefit of all parties, and the tenant for life is entitled only upon this principle : thus wasting property is converted for the benefit of persons in remainder, future interests for the benefit of the tenant for life.

Notes.—But the testator may by his will shew an intention that the property as it then exists shall be specifically enjoyed, and the Court rather leans in favour of this construction so far as it is consistent with the decision in the above case. Where perishable, wasting, or reversionary property is given to persons in succession *specifically*, in the strict sense of the word, then there can be no reason for converting it ; and if an intention can be collected from the will, that property shall be enjoyed in specie, as it existed at the death of the testator, although the property be not, in a technical sense, specifically bequeathed, it will not be converted.

The rule laid down in the case of *Howe* v. *Earl of Dartmouth* has been stated as follows :—" Where personal estate is given in terms amounting to a general residuary bequest to be enjoyed by persons in succession, the interpretation the Court puts upon the bequest is that the persons indicated are to enjoy the same thing in succession, and in order to effectuate that intention the Court, as a general rule, converts into permanent investments so much of the personalty as is of a wasting or perishable nature at the death of the testator, and also reversionary interests. The rule did not originally ascribe to testators the intention to effect such conversions except in so far as a testator may be supposed to intend that which the law will do ; but the Court, finding the intention of the testator to be that the object of his bounty shall take successive interests in one and the same thing converts the property as the only means of giving effect to that intention" (2 Lead. Cas. Eq. 310).

HOOLEY v. HATTON.

(2 *Lead. Cas. Eq.* 321.)

(1 *Bro. C. C.* 390, *n.*)

Lady Finch, by her will, gave the plaintiff a legacy of
£500, and afterwards, by a codicil, a legacy of £1,000 ;
and the question was, whether the last legacy alone
passed, or the legatee should have both.

Decided :—That the plaintiff was entitled to both
legacies ; but that if a legacy of the same amount is
given twice for the same cause and in the same act, and
in the same or nearly the same words, then it will *not*
be double ; but where in *different* writings there is a
bequest of equal, greater, or less sums, it is an augmentation.

Notes.—Although it would appear from this case that if the
legacies are given by different instruments, they will never be
considered as a repetition, yet this is not quite so, for even then
if they are for the same sum *and* the same motive, the Court
presumes that they are but a repetition, but both these coin-
cidences must exist.

It is important to observe whether extrinsic evidence can be
given to shew whether a testator intended a legacy to be by
way of augmentation or as a repetition, as if so the rules laid
down in the above case might often be altered, and it is established on this point that where the Court raises the presumption
against double legacies it will receive parol evidence to shew
that the testator actually intended the double gift he has expressed, for that but rebuts the presumption of the Court, and

supports the apparent intention of the will; but where the Court raises no presumption, as where legacies are given by different instruments, it will not admit parol evidence to shew testator only meant the legatee to take one, for that would be to contradict the will (2 Lead. Cas. Eq. 326).

EX PARTE PYE.
(2 *Lead. Cas. Eq.* 338.)
(18 *Ves.* 140.)

Decided :—1. That as a general rule, where a parent gives a legacy to a child, not stating the purpose with reference to which he gives it, he is understood to give a portion; and in consequence of the leaning against double portions, if the parent afterwards advances a portion on the marriage of the child, the presumption arises that it was intended to be a satisfaction of the legacy either wholly or in part; and this applies where a person puts himself *in loco parentis.*

2. But no such presumption arises in the case of a stranger or of a natural child, where the donor has *not* put himself *in loco parentis,* unless the subsequent advance is proved to be for the very purpose of satisfying the legacy; and therefore the legatee will be entitled to both.

TALBOT v. DUKE OF SHREWSBURY.
(2 *Lead. Cas. Eq.* 352.)
(*Prec. Ch.* 394.)

Decided :—That if a debtor, without taking notice of the debt, bequeaths a sum as great as, or greater than, the debt, to his creditor, this is a satisfaction; but it is not a satisfaction if it is bequeathed on a contingency, or if it were less than the debt.

CHANCEY'S CASE.

(2 *Lead. Cas. Eq.* 353.)
(1 *P. Wms.* 408.)

Testator during his lifetime, and before making his will, gave his servant a bond for £100. He afterwards made his will and bequeathed her £500, *and directed that all his debts and legacies should be paid.*

Decided :—That the legacy was not here a satisfaction of the debt, because it was attended with particular circumstances varying it from the common rule, for the testator had directed that all his debts and legacies should be paid.

Notes on these three Cases.—These three cases are all authorities on, and illustrations of, the doctrine of satisfaction, which may be defined as the giving by a person liable to some claim of the donee. of something different from the subject of such claim, but intended in substitution thereof. The first case given above is as to satisfaction of legacies by portions, and the latter two are as to satisfaction of debts by legacies. It is important to remember the great difference that exists in satisfaction in the case of portions on the one hand, and in the case of legacies to creditors on the other; for in the first case Equity, leaning against double portions, is in favour of the satisfaction, so that where there is a legacy to or a settlement on a child, and a subsequent advancement on the marriage of such child, such advancement will be a satisfaction altogether if of the same or a greater amount, and if of a less amount it will be a satisfaction *pro tanto;* but in the second case it is just the opposite, for Equity will take hold of slight circumstances to rebut the presumption of satisfaction that would otherwise arise. This is well exemplified by *Chancey's Case;* and another case that may be usefully referred to on the point is that of *Clark* v. *Sewell* (3 Atk. 96), where there was a legacy given to a creditor far exceeding the amount of the debt, but the legacies were directed to be paid *one month* after testator's decease, and it was held that the fact of the legacies not being payable till after a month prevented the satisfaction which would otherwise have taken place. Indeed in this class of cases satisfaction will never occur unless the legacy given to the creditor is equal to or greater in amount than the debt, and in every possible respect equally beneficial, and also provided that no intention appears that it is not to be a satisfaction.

The principle upon which the Court leans against double portions is founded upon the idea that the parent or person *in loco parentis* fixes the amount of the portion or provision for the child, and that any benefit he afterwards gives is on account of the obligation which he would otherwise have discharged at his death, and this explains why the doctrine has no operation in the case of persons towards whom the testator occupied no such relationship.

Satisfaction is sometimes styled ademption, and students are apt to get confused between cases of ademption and satisfaction, a matter which has been well explained thus :—" When the will is made first, and the settlement afterwards, it is always treated as a case of what is called ademption—that is to say, the benefits given by the settlement are considered to be an ademption of the same benefits given to the same child by the will. With reference to cases . . . . of a previous settlement and a subsequent will . . . . it is now quite settled that there is no difference between the two cases beyond the verbal difference that the term satisfaction is used where the settlement has preceded the will, and the term ademption where the will has preceded the settlement. In substance there is no distinction between the principles applied to the two classes of cases." (*Coventry* v.

Chichester, 2 H. & M. 159, quoted in Snell's Principles of Equity, 6th ed. 240, note (*y*).)

With regard to the admissibility of extrinsic evidence on the point of satisfaction, the rule against double portions is a presumption of law, and like other presumptions of law may be rebutted by evidence of extrinsic circumstances. To vary or contradict the plain effect of a document where there is no presumption of law contrary to that effect, extrinsic evidence is not admissible; but to confirm the plain effect of a document where there is a presumption of law contrary to that effect, extrinsic evidence is admissible (Snell's Principles of Equity, 6th ed. 250–252).

WILCOCKS v. WILCOCKS.

(2 *Lead. Cas. Eq.* 389.)

(2 *Vern.* 558.)

The plaintiff's father, upon his marriage, covenanted to purchase lands of the value of £200 per annum, and settle the same upon himself for life and to his first and other sons in tail. He purchased lands of that value, but made no settlement or disposition thereof, so that they descended to the plaintiff as heir-at-law.

Decided :—That the plaintiff was not entitled to specific performance of the covenant, but that the lands descended must be taken as a performance or satisfaction thereof, and therefore the covenant was already performed.

BLANDY v. WIDMORE.

(2 *Lead. Cas. Eq.* 391.)

(1 *P. Wms.* 323.)

In marriage articles the husband covenanted to leave his wife £620 if she should survive him. He died intestate, and the wife's share, under the Statute of Distributions, far exceeded £620.

Decided :—That the wife was *not* entitled to have the £620 *and* her distributive share, but the distributive share must be taken as a satisfaction or performance of the covenant.

Notes on these two Cases.—The doctrine of "performance," which is illustrated by the above cases, bears rather closely on that of satisfaction; but on a very short consideration of the subject, and a comparison of the cases on satisfaction (see *ante*, pp. 110, 111) with those above given on performance, the distinction will be obvious. That distinction has been stated to be that "satisfaction implies the substitution or gift of something different from the thing agreed to be given, but equivalent to it in the eye of the law, while in cases of performance the thing agreed to be done is in truth wholly or in part performed." *Wilcocks* v. *Wilcocks* and *Blandy* v. *Widmore* exemplify the maxim, which is shortly stated as "Equity imputes an intention to fulfil an obligation." In *Wilcocks* v. *Wilcocks* it will be seen that the lands there purchased were of equal value with those covenanted to be settled, but it has also been decided that even where the lands purchased are of less value, they shall be considered as in part performance of the covenant (*Lechmere* v. *Earl of Carlisle*, 3 Peere Wms. 211). Where the covenant points to a *future* purchase of lands it cannot be presumed that lands of which the covenantor was seised at the time of the covenant were intended to be taken in performance or part performance of it; nor can it be presumed that property of a different nature from that covenanted to be purchased was intended as a performance. Although by the settlement the consent of the trustees is required, still the absence of that consent will not necessarily prevent the presumption of performance from arising, if the other circumstances of the purchase are favourable to such presumption (Snell's Principles of Equity, 6th ed. 228).

It should be mentioned that it has been decided that although a distributive share on an intestacy will be taken as performance of a covenant, yet a gift by will of a sum of money as a residue will not so operate *per se*, because it imports bounty. And where the covenant is not to pay a gross sum, but the interest of a sum of money for life or a mere life annuity, the principle upon which *Blandy* v. *Widmore* was decided does not apply.

EYRE v. COUNTESS OF SHAFTESBURY.

(2 Lead. Cas. Eq. 633.)
(2 P. Wms. 103.)

The former Earl of Shaftesbury, by his will, gave the guardianship of his infant son to the plaintiff and two others since deceased, without expressing that it was to be to the survivor of them, and the plaintiff now prayed that the infant (who was in his mother's custody) might be delivered up to him as his guardian.

Decided:—That though the guardianship was only given to the three persons without saying " and to the survivors or survivor of them," yet the survivor—the plaintiff—should have it.

Afterwards, when the infant was of the age of fourteen years, his mother the Countess procured his marriage with one Lady Susannah Noel, without the consent or privity of the plaintiff, the guardian.

Decided:—That the Countess was liable for a contempt of Court, although the marriage was in other respects proper.

Notes.—There are properly six species of guardianship—viz.: (1) By nature; (2) By nurture; (3) In socage; (4) By statute; (5) By appointment of the Court; (6) *Ad litem.* There is also guardianship by custom, and the quite obsolete species of guardianship by election (see Stephen's Com. 9th ed. vol. ii. pp. 310–315).

The above is the leading case on the nature of the guardianship and the guardian's powers under the statute of 12 Car. 2, c. 24.

That statute gives the *father* (a) the power by deed executed in writing, or by his last will and testament, to appoint the custody and tuition of such of his children as at the time of his death are neither of full age nor married until they attain the age of twenty-one years, or during any less period. This power, however, does not apply to illegitimate children (*Sleeman* v. *Wilson*, L. R. 13 Eq. 36). This statute of course only gives the power to the *father;* but a stranger may to a certain extent appoint a guardian, for such an appointment will be effectual if there is a legacy to the father conditional on his giving up the guardianship, which legacy the father elects to take, or if it is manifestly for the benefit of the infant, and the duty of the father to acquiesce in the appointment; but the benefit to the infant must be a solid consideration, and not merely expectation.

By statute 2 & 3 Vict. c. 54, it was provided that judges in Equity might make orders on petition for the access of mothers to their infant children, and if such children were within the age of seven years for delivery of them into the mother's custody until attaining such age of seven years; but no order was to be made under such provision in favour of a mother against whom adultery had been established. This statute is now repealed by the 36 Vict. c. 12, which in lieu thereof provides (sect. 1) that the Court of Chancery may order mothers to have access to or custody or control of their children until they shall attain such age as the Court shall direct, not exceeding the age of sixteen.

Provision is also made by the Divorce Act (20 & 21 Vict. c. 85, sect. 35) enabling the Divorce Court, in any divorce, judicial separation, or nullity of marriage proceedings, to make such provision as it may deem just and proper with respect to the custody, maintenance, and education of the children, the marriage of whose parents is the subject of the proceedings. And by the Matrimonial Causes Act, 1878 (41 Vict. c. 19, sect. 4) it is provided that on a magistrate making an order under that Act which is to

(a) The above statute gives this power to the father, whether he is of full age or not; but now, as by the Wills Act (1 Vict. c. 26) an infant cannot make a valid will, he cannot appoint a guardian by will, but only by deed (2 Lead. Cas. Eq. 661).

have the effect of a judical separation between husband and wife,
he may also give to the wife the custody of the children of the
marriage up to the age of 10 years.

It is also provided by 36 Vict. c. 12, s. 2, that no agreement
in a separation deed for the father giving up the custody of his
children to the mother shall be invalid, but the same is not to
be enforced by the Court if it is of opinion that it will not be
for the benefit of the infant or infants to give effect to it.
Formerly the rule was that he could not contract away the
obligation with regard to his children thrown upon him by the
law, unless he had been guilty of such gross misconduct as
totally to unfit him to have their custody and control—when in
fact the Court, on being applied to, would have deprived him of
their custody (*Swift* v. *Swift*, 34 Beav. 266).

STAPILTON v. STAPILTON.

(2 *Lead. Cas. Eq.* 836.)

(1 *Atk.* 2.)

Decided :—That an agreement entered into upon a supposition of a right, or of a doubtful right, though it afterwards appears that the right was on the other side, shall be binding, and the right shall not prevail against the agreement of the parties ; for the right must always be on one side or the other, and therefore the compromise of a doubtful right is a sufficient foundation of an agreement.

That where agreements are entered into to save the honour of a family, and are reasonable ones, a Court of Equity will, if possible, decree a performance of them.

GORDON v. GORDON.

(3 *Swanst.* 400.)

Here there had been an agreement between two brothers for the settlement of the family estates, as the younger disputed the elder's legitimacy. At the time of the agreement, however, the younger brother was aware of a private marriage that had taken place, and this was not communicated to the other. The legitimacy of the elder brother was afterwards established, and, although some nineteen years had elapsed,

Decided :—That the agreement must be rescinded because of the concealment by the younger brother of the fact of the private marriage, and that it mattered not whether the omission to disclose it originated in design or in an honest opinion of the invalidity of the ceremony and a want of obligation on his part to make the communication.

Notes on these two Cases.—The rule as to family compromises is laid down in Snell's Principles of Equity (6th ed. 432), thus :— "In order that a family arrangement may be supported there must be a full and fair communication of all material circumstances affecting the subject-matter of the agreement which are within the knowledge of the several parties, whether such information be asked for by the other party or not. There must not only be good faith and honest intention, but full disclosure; and without full disclosure honest intention is not sufficient.

Stapilton v. *Stapilton* is given in Messrs. White and Tudor's book as the leading case on this subject; but the facts and decision in *Gordon* v. *Gordon* are also given above, as it is thought that case constitutes a more forcible illustration of the subject.

BRICE v. STOKES.

(2 *Lead. Cas. Eq.* 865.)
(11 *Ves.* 319.)

The question in this case was, whether a trustee should be charged with certain purchase-money, which, though he had joined in the receipt, had been received by his co-trustee.

Decided :—That *under the particular circumstances* of the case he was liable to be charged, the sale being unnecessary, and he permitting his co-trustee to keep and act with the money contrary to the trust; but that he should not be charged in respect of the interest of one of the *cestuis que trust* who had notice of the breach of trust and acquiesced therein.

Notes.—This case also lays down the law as to the distinction between receipts of trustees and executors, but as it can hardly be considered altogether correct at the present day, this part of the decision has not been stated. So far as it is possible from the numerous cases on the subject to collect a clear rule, it may be stated that in the case of trustees joining in receipts, as they have but a joint authority, and their joining is therefore necessary for conformity, no presumption of receipt of the money will usually exist; but in the case of executors, as they ordinarily have not merely a joint but also a several power, if they have joined in signing the receipt a presumption of actual receipt of the money arises. But this presumption may be rebutted by shewing that in fact the particular executor did not receive the money.

Although, as shown in the principal case, a trustee is safe in permitting his co-trustee to receive the money, if he merely joins for conformity, yet the rule goes no further than this; for if he allows the money to remain in his co-trustee's hands for a longer time than the circumstances of the case reasonably require, he will be liable for any misapplication.

Brice v. *Stokes* is also, as appears above, an authority to shew that acquiescence in a breach of trust discharges a trustee. But persons under disability, as married women and infants, are not ordinarily bound by an acquiescence, release, or confirmation, except in the case of a *feme covert* as to property held by her to her separate use, and which she is not restrained from anticipating.

PENN v. LORD BALTIMORE.

(2 *Lead. Cas. Eq.* 930.)

(1 *Ves.* 444.)

Here the plaintiff and defendant being in England, had entered into articles for settling the boundaries of two provinces in America—Pennsylvania and Maryland—and the plaintiff sought a specific performance of the articles. The principal objection was that the property was out of the jurisdiction of the Court.

Decided :—That the plaintiff was entitled to specific performance of the articles, for though the Court had no original jurisdiction on the direct question of the original right of the boundaries, the property being abroad, yet that did not at all matter, as the suit was founded on the articles, and the Court acted *in personam.*

Notes.—The above case forms a good illustration of the well-known maxim or principle, "Equity acts *in personam ;*" a maxim which indeed shews the great difference in the jurisdiction of Equity to that of Law : thus at Law the only remedy on a breach of contract was an action for damages; but in Equity, as the Court acted *in personam,* the party could always when proper, be compelled to do the very act. So in this case, although the property was abroad, and therefore the Court really in respect of the property had no jurisdiction, yet the parties being here, the Court was able to award the appropriate remedy, acting not at all on the property but directly on the persons.

PEACHEY v. DUKE OF SOMERSET.

(2 *Lead. Cas. Eq.* 1100.)

(1 *Stra.* 447.)

Here the plaintiff was tenant of copyhold lands in a manor of which the defendant was lord. He committed acts of forfeiture by making leases contrary to the custom, without licence, and by felling timber, &c., and he now brought this suit, offering to make compensation and praying relief from the forfeitures.

Decided :—That the plaintiff was *not* entitled to relief; and that the true ground of relief against penalties is from the original intent of the case, where the penalty is designed only to secure money, and the Court can give by way of recompense all that was expected or desired.

SLOMAN v. WALTER.

(2 *Lead. Cas. Eq.* 1112.)

(1 *Bro. C. C.* 418.)

The plaintiff and defendant were partners in the Chapter Coffee House, and it had been agreed that defendant should have the use of a particular room when he wanted it, and the plaintiff gave a bond to secure this. Upon breach of the agreement, defendant brought an action for the penalty of the bond, and the plaintiff brought this suit for an injunction, and for the actual damage sustained by defendant to be assessed.

Decided :—That plaintiff was entitled to an injunction, and that the rule is, that where a penalty is inserted merely to secure the enjoyment of a *collateral object,* the enjoyment of the object is considered as the principal intent of the deed, and the penalty only as additional and to secure the damages really incurred.

Notes on these two Cases.—The relief given by the Court in the case of penalties and forfeitures furnishes a good illustration of the maxim, " Equity regards the spirit and not the letter." The rule as to when Equity will relieve in such cases is well stated in the latter of the above two decisions, whilst the former shews an instance beyond the relief of Equity. It should be observed also that *Sloman* v. *Walter* shews that the jurisdiction of Equity as to relief against penalties is not so limited as to extend only to those penalties intended to secure payment of a sum of money, as might appear from *Peachey* v. *Duke of Somerset,* but that it also extends to penalties to secure *performance of some collateral act.*

Care must be taken to distinguish between a penalty and a sum which is really liquidated damages ; not that it follows that because parties stipulate that a sum shall be paid on breach of a contract "as and for liquidated damages" the Court will always so consider the sum, for notwithstanding it is so called, it may be a penalty in the disguise of liquidated damages (see *Kemble* v. *Farren,* 6 Bing. 141). But where the sum stipulated to be paid is really and in fact liquidated damages, then the Court will not interfere. The question of liquidated damages or a penalty is, however, one very often most difficult to determine, and depends upon the construction of the whole instrument taken together.

The doctrines of Chancery in giving relief in the case of penalties and forfeitures are not now peculiar to the Chancery Division, but the same construction will be put with regard to them in all Divisions of the Court (Judicature Act, 1873, sect. 25 (7); 2 Lead. Cas. Eq. 1139, 1140).

By reason of the Conveyancing Act, 1881 (44 & 45 Vict. c. 41, sect. 14), a right of re-entry or forfeiture under a lease is not enforceable until service on the lessee of a notice specifying the breach; and if capable of remedy, requiring the lessee to remedy it; and in any case requiring the lessee to make compensation in damages for the breach, and the lessee fails within a reasonable time to conform with the notice. The Court has also full power of granting relief against the forfeiture. This provision does not, however, extend to a covenant or condition against assigning, underletting, or parting with the land, or to a condition for forfeiture on bankruptcy or execution, nor in the case of a mining lease to a covenant or condition for access or inspection of books, accounts, weighing-machines, &c. Also it does not affect the law relating to forfeiture for non-payment of rent, as to which the Court of Chancery at an early date assumed jurisdiction to give relief within six months, and by the Common Law Procedure Act, 1860 (23 & 24 Vict. c. 126, sect. 1), it is provided that in an action of ejectment similar relief may be given.

LANSDOWNE v. LANSDOWNE.

(2 *Jacob & Walker*, 205.)

In this case the plaintiff, who was a son of the eldest brother of a deceased intestate, had a dispute with his uncle, a younger brother, respecting the right to inherit the real estate of the deceased. They referred the matter to a schoolmaster, who, acting on the axiom, " Land cannot ascend, but always descends," awarded in favour of the uncle (the younger brother).

This bill was filed by the son of the elder brother to be relieved.

Decided :—That the plaintiff was entitled to relief, and decreed accordingly, notwithstanding the maxim, *Ignorantia legis non excusat.*

EARL BEAUCHAMP v. WINN.

(*L. R. 6 Eng. & Ir. App.* 223.)

The late Earl Beauchamp and the defendant had entered into an exchange of property, including a certain warren of conics, both proceeding upon the belief that the Earl had only the right of warren over the lands, and that defendant had the right to the lands themselves. Subsequently the original lease was found, and the Earl considered that it passed to him not merely the right of warren, but the right to the land itself. This suit was commenced to rescind the agreement for exchange as being entered into in mutual ignorance and mistake. It was held by the judges that the words in the lease did not carry the soil, but only the right of warren; but had it been otherwise, relief might have been given to the plaintiff; and the following points on the subject of mistake were laid down :—

1. Where in the making of an agreement between two parties there has been a mutual mistake as to their rights occasioning an injury to one of them, the rule of Equity is in favour of interposing to grant relief.

2. Although the parties have subsequently to the agreement dealt with the property, or other circumstances have intervened, so that it may be difficult to restore them to their original condition, the Court will not, if a ground for relief is established, decline to grant such relief.

3. The rule, *Ignorantia legis non excusat*, though applying where the alleged ignorance is that of a well-known rule of law, does *not* so apply where the mistake is of a matter of law arising upon the doubtful construction of a grant.

4. Acquiescence in what has been done will not be a bar to relief where the party alleged to have acquiesced has acted, or abstained from acting 'through being ignorant that he possessed rights which would be available against that which he permitted to be enjoyed.

Notes.—A mistake as remediable in Equity is defined by Mr. Snell in his Principles of Equity as "some unintentional act, or omission, or error, arising from ignorance, surprise, imposition, or misplaced confidence" (6th. ed. 429).

It is usually said that "*Ignorantia facti excusat*," but "*Ignorantia legis non excusat*;" but these two simple maxims do not at all adequately answer the question, When will Equity give relief in cases of mistake ?   This is, indeed, a question rather difficult to answer properly in a short space ; but the law on the subject seems to be as follows :—Mistakes may be divided into (1) Mistakes in matters of fact, and (2) Mistakes in matters of law ; and as to the latter no relief will be given, *except* where the mistake is one of title arising from ignorance of a principle of law of such constant occurrence as to be supposed to be understood by the community at large.   The case of *Lansdowne* v. *Lansdowne* given above is on this exception, the reason of which is, that a mistake in such a matter affords a conclusive presumption of ignorance, imposition, or the like.   The rule of " *Ignorantia legis non excusat*" also does not apply where the mistake is of a matter of law arising upon some point of doubtful construction, for the ignorance before a decision of what was the true construction, cannot deprive a person of his right to relief.   It is very different to a well-known rule of law (see *Earl Beauchamp v. Winn*, *supra*).

But the other class—viz., mistakes in matters of fact—may be divided as of two kinds : (1) Where the mistake consists in having done something under an erroneous impression ; and (2) Where it consists in having done something never intended to be done. In the latter kind of cases relief will almost universally be given, but in the former it is far more difficult to obtain relief, and more usually it will not be granted, though in some cases it will ; for instance, when the mistake consists in supposing the existence of something which in point of fact does not exist.   The mistake must generally be unilateral only, unless founded on mutual surprise.   Acquiescence in a mistake will deprive a person of any right to be relieved against it.   In *Earl Beauchamp v. Winn* the alleged mistake had existed for more than sixty years, and it was argued in that case that the appellant was barred by his acquiescence, which might be implied from length of time, but it was decided that the ignorance of the appellant prevented any acquiescence on his part.

"In regard to mistakes in wills there is no doubt that Courts of Equity have jurisdiction to correct them when they are apparent on the face of the will, or may be made out by a due construction of its terms, for in all cases of wills the intention will prevail over the words. But then the mistake must be apparent on the face of the will, otherwise there can be no relief; for parol evidence or evidence *dehors* the will is not admissible to vary or control the terms of the will, although it is admissible to remove a latent ambiguity" (Snell's Principles of Equity, 6th ed. 440).

GENERAL INDEX.

A.

D.

E.

Portions : *See* " Satisfaction or Ademption."
> Not to be raised if the party dies, though in similar cases a
> legacy might be, 43

Powers,
> Excessive execution of, 16–18
> If execution excessive, part may be good, and excess only
> bad, 16–18
> Equity will assist in case of defective execution, 16–18
> But not in the case of non-execution except in two cases, 16–18
> Special power must be executed *bonâ fide*, 17, 18
> Doctrine of *cy-près* with regard to excessive execution of
> powers, 18
> Of three kinds, 18
> Also general and special, 18
> Illusory applications under, 19
> Provisions of Conveyancing Act, 1881, as to disclaiming or
> releasing, 19
> Liability of person purchasing under power of sale to see to
> application of purchase-money, 59, 60

Precatory Trusts,
> When created, 20
> Recommendation must be imperative, 20
> The subject and object of recommendation must be certain, 20
> Are properly styled express trusts, 21

Prescription,
> Former law, and present position as to, 8, 9

Prospect,
> Right to, cannot be acquired by prescription, 11

Public Parks Act, the, 27, 28

Purchase,
> By one person in the name of another, generally as to, 63–65
> Such a purchase forms good instance of an implied trust, 65

Purchaser,
> His liability to see to application of purchase-money before
> statutes, 59, 60
> Trustees, powers of giving receipt to, under 22 & 23 Vict.
> c. 35, and 44 & 45 Vict. c. 41, 59, 60
> This latter Act retrospective, 59
> No discovery against purchaser without notice, 89

R.

Receipts by Trustees : *See* Trustees ; Executors.

Reconversion,
> Definition and instance of, 101

Wild's case,
    The rule in, and generally as to, 31, 32

Wills,
    When the Court will relieve in the case of mistakes in, 130

Y.

Year to Year,
    Distinction between tenancy from year to year and at will,
        1, 2
    Notice to be given to determine tenancy from year to year, 2

THE END.

PRINTED BY BALLANTYNE, HANSON AND CO.
LONDON AND EDINBURGH

www.ingramcontent.com/pod-product-compliance
Lightning Source LLC
Chambersburg PA
CBHW020016030726
47500CB00002B/614